MW01282980

This book is a work o places, and incidents are products of the writer's imagination or have been used fictitiously and are not to be construed as real. Any resemblance to persons, living or dead, actual events, locale or organizations is entirely coincidental.

Wild West Series

Wes Roshannon, bounty hunter extraordinaire, always gets his man, but he's having a tough time looking for the father he never knew. A lead takes him to the doorstep of a local, very private biker club where admittance is exclusive. And can be downright dangerous. Wes is used to putting it all on the line, until he's blindsided by a vision with long dark hair and flashing eyes.

Stormy thought she was content living in the shadow of the Bighorns giving her dad's biker club its name, wrapped in the safety of a group she's come to think of as family. That's until the big man, asking questions and raking her with his steel gray eyes, has her thinking of living her life on her own terms, away from watchful eyes and parental concern.

Wes is far too involved with the gorgeous brunette to be intimidated by her biker family, and not even her growly, overbearing father will keep Wes away from her. But when he hunts a bail jumper right to the club's front door, he's torn between love, loyalty and the law.

Something About a Bounty Hunter

by

Em Petrova

Chapter One

If there was one thing Aunt Winter didn't approve of it was Wes's motorcycle parked in the driveway. She said the engine spooked the chickens and they wouldn't lay the following day. She claimed the horses were bad-tempered after Wes drove "that thing."

But none of it was true. She just hated what his motorcycle meant and associated it with losing her sister.

Halfway up the driveway to the ranch, he cut the engine and swung his leg over to walk the bike in so Aunt Winter didn't have anything to complain about. He hadn't been home in too long and he wasn't out to cause trouble.

He dragged in a deep breath of the ranch air, a mix of country living mixed with the mountains. He could never put words to what it smelled like other than home, and he was glad to be here.

The big house where he'd grown up with his twin cousins was unchanged. Same with the barn. But one of the outbuildings had a new roof, which only gave him a sore spot in his chest that could only be guilt.

He should have been here to help with the roof. Hopefully one of his cousins had assisted Uncle Matthias in the construction.

As he approached the house, he heard the low cluck of Aunt Winter's chickens. Since he and his cousins had grown and moved out, she treated those chickens like kids, spoiling them on special grain and even talking to them in baby voices. She said it made them lay the biggest, best eggs, but he knew better. She missed the boys she'd raised — and that gave him more of a guilt complex.

Using the heel of his heavy black boots, he flipped down the kickstand and ensured his bike was safely balanced before turning for the house.

A welcoming front porch and many windows in the front of the home beckoned. The thought of home-cooking reminded his stomach he was at Eagle Crest too.

The door opened and his aunt stepped onto the porch, hand to her brow, shielding her eyes against the bright spring sun.

"Hello, Aunt Winter." His voice was dusky from thirst and disuse. He'd been riding too long. His search had taken him far this time.

Her jaw dropped and then she leaped off the porch steps like a schoolgirl. He caught her as she threw her arms around his neck. "Oh, my dear Wes! I thought I heard that motorcycle engine, but then it stopped and I wondered if I'd imagined it. It's been *so* long since you've been home."

He hugged her hard, aware that she was rounder than he'd last seen her but the same old aunt who'd raised him like a son.

She planted a kiss on his cheek and stepped back to look at him.

Study him, more like. She started at his heavy boots, not cowboy boots, and moved to his leather chaps, not his worn jeans, up to leather jacket, not his plaid shirt, and ending at his helmet. Most definitely not his black Stetson.

She made a sound like a sigh.

"I like you better in your hat. I think there's one upstairs in your closet."

He had to admit he preferred his hat too. He couldn't count the times he reached to tug on the brim, only to find his head bare. Living among bikers, he wanted to fit in. Turning up like the cowboy he was wouldn't have many doors opening to him, and he definitely would not be getting the answers he'd been seeking these many months.

"I've got my hat in my saddlebag. I'll wear it to dinner."

She slapped at his arm. "Oh you will not wear it to the table. You know better!"

He chuckled.

"Teaser. Always trying to give me heart attacks your entire childhood, I swear. But I must have done something right—look how you turned out. If anything, I fed you well." She gave his six-two frame another once-over.

"I'm glad to be home. Where's Uncle Matthias?"

She waved at the ranch. "You know him. Could be checking the herd at this time of day. Why don't you get changed and then ride out and see if you can bring him back for dinner?"

He knew her suggestion was partly for selfish reasons. She hated seeing him in biker garb, and he had to admit those soft, worn jeans and flannel shirt sounded good about now. He grabbed his stuff out of the saddlebag and then followed her inside.

"How're Judd and Aiden?" He kept in touch with his cousins. As a bounty hunter, Wes needed info on bail jumpers at times and Judd and Aiden, both lawmen, sometimes helped out.

"Your cousins are well. Their wives too. Amaryllis is about to pop out that baby any minute and still the woman refuses to stay home. She goes with Aiden on every single call."

Aiden and Amaryllis shared a passion for investigating cattle thefts around the state and Wes could see her dragging a baby along with them once it was born.

"And Judd and Cecily?" he prompted.

"No baby bumps in sight yet." Aunt Winter *tsked* like it was a crime they didn't have another grandbaby in the chute yet.

"All in good time," Wes said. She stepped aside and he put his foot on the bottom step leading up to his bedroom. "They coming up this weekend?"

Aunt Winter's eyes twinkled, and he thought he spotted a tear in the corner of one. Now that made him feel *really* bad. He needed to make a better effort to come home more often. It was too easy to get caught up in his own life. Between hunting fugitives and his personal searches of every motorcycle club in the tristate area, he didn't have a lot of down time.

"The whole crew will be home for dinner. I am a happy woman." She eyed Wes. "I'll be happier to see you in your own clothes."

"These *are* my own clothes," he said gently. He understood why she hated the bikers—she blamed them for taking her sister, Wes's mother, and turning her away from her family. In the end, she'd died far from home and Aunt Winter had never forgiven the bikers for it.

Before she could comment more on his leather, he started up the stairs. "I'll change and then go find Uncle Matthias."

A few minutes later he slipped outside without his aunt fussing over his appearance. His comfortable Stetson shaded his eyes and he hardly had to squint into the sun as he strode to the barn.

The scents of horse and hay brought a smile to his face and his shoulders relaxed. He went down the line of stalls, greeting each horse there. They'd been well-exercised all morning and were now getting comfy. But his favorite mare was always up for a gallop.

He opened the stall door and she pushed forward, nudging him hard in the shoulder. He reached up to stroke her mane. "I know I haven't been here to ride you much, have I? I'm sorry."

The horse answered with a soft whicker. While he tacked her up to ride, the animal stood completely still, patiently waiting. He led her out the door and swung into the saddle. A whoop gathered in his chest but he didn't release the sound. Instead, he put his boots to flanks and took off across the field.

He rode for ten minutes, looping around the land and just staring at the steel-blue mountains in the distance. Being on horseback was an entirely different rush from being on two wheels. Though in his mind, they were equal.

He loved the bikers he'd met and lived with. He might not have found his father among them yet, but he had no doubt he'd eventually locate him. He wasn't a legend for hunting men for nothing. Not many people could hide from Wes. If only his aunt would come clean with him and tell him exactly which club his mother had belonged to, he'd be able to find his father in a blink.

Aunt Winter was beyond stubborn on that front, and Wes had learned that pushing caused her pain.

Up ahead, he caught the jingle of a harness, the sound carrying back to him on the breeze. He lay over the horse's neck and kicked it up into high gear. Running flat out through the high grasses that whispered with each hoofbeat. His own pulse added to the music of home.

When he caught up to his uncle, he found himself smiling. After a tense week of trying to get a group of bikers to trust him enough to give him answers about his father, he'd managed to get three fugitives back into custody. Damn, he needed this time to unwind.

Though he'd count it as one of his busier weeks, it was nothing as rough as his stint in the government. Top secret, talk-and-be-killed stuff. No one in his family knew about his time in Operation Freedom Flag, but he suspected Judd knew. As sheriff, he had access to a lot of intel and lawmen talked to other lawmen.

He turned his thoughts to what his uncle was doing out here. Matthias circled the back of the herd once, twice.

Wes crossed the field toward him, and his uncle looked up. Surprise lit his face, and he gave Wes a big smile that was more welcome than he deserved for one day.

"Hey, Wes. Wasn't expectin' ya."

"Didn't think to call. What's going on up here? Dinner's almost ready."

"I know fine what time your aunt gets dinner on the table. I thought I saw one of the young'uns limping. I keep looking closely, but as soon as I see it, I think I'm imagining things."

"I'll take a look." Wes held the reins loosely, easing his mare forward. He rode in an arc behind the cattle, watching their feet for the limp Matthias had mentioned.

"That one there with a white spot on its rump." His uncle pointed.

Wes looked closer. After the animal took three or four steps, he thought he saw it. A misstep.

"That's odd, isn't it?" He scratched his jaw, the five o'clock shadow rasping under his thumbnail.

Matthias dipped his head in a nod. "Sure is. Thinkin' I should pull her out, examine her closer."

Wes set his hand over the coil of rope clipped to his belt. "I'll do it."

"You?"

Wes stared at him. "What's wrong with me doin' it?"

"You've gotta be rusty. When was the last time you roped a cow?"

"Been a while, but I roped a fugitive who was running from me last week."

Matthias chuckled and waved at the cow. "Be my guest, then. Just don't miss. She won't stand there pretty for you very long."

Wes grunted and lifted the rope. The familiar motion of throwing a lasso came as naturally to him as walking. When he tossed, a shrill whistle sounded and he came up short. His rope hit the young cow's back and slipped off.

"Damn." He looked around to see two more riders—Judd and Aiden—making their way across the field to meet them.

Crap, they'd seen him miss. He was never going to live it down.

Matthias gave him a crooked grin, the same Wes had adopted as his own over the years. His uncle was his role model, and he couldn't have asked for a better one. Except he wasn't his father. Wes wished it didn't matter. Had spent a lifetime trying to convince himself that his uncle's affection was enough. But the fact was, he had to find his roots. There was no other option for him.

His cousins reined up with twin shit-eating grins on their identical faces. "I see you haven't improved your rope skills, Wes," Aiden teased.

"You're lucky I don't have my taser on me," he grumbled.

Aiden gave him a bored look. "Dude, we've all taken turns using the taser on each other, but it was you who pissed your pants."

"I'm pretty sure we were fifteen when we got ahold of that taser. I'm a lot older and bigger now." Wes only had some inches on his cousins but a hell of a lot more bulk. As a kid he'd been bullied, and his cousins had always stuck up for him. He'd vowed the minute he was old enough that he'd start putting on muscle. And he hadn't just put it on—he'd *packed* it on.

He looped his rope again and made the toss, landing it square over the cow's ears. He gave a yank to tighten the rope and then threw his cousins a smug look. He lazily dismounted from his horse to walk up to the cow.

The herd skittered away at his approach. He inspected the leg, careful to stay out of reach of the hooves. When he glanced up, his cousins were grinning at him.

"Assholes," he said with only the highest affection for them. "Least you could do is compliment me on that throw."

"What throw? That piddly little toss you made? Hell, I'd call it dumb luck, wouldn't you, Aiden?" Judd patted his mount's neck.

"Pathetic," Aiden added, always playing along with his brother's game.

Uncle Matthias chuckled. "Good to have you boys home. We'd best get on back before your aunt squawks like one of her chickens about us being late to dinner. Wes, you need a hand leading that cow home?"

He snorted at his uncle's jab. "Not you too." Wes shook his head but couldn't stop the smile from spreading over his face. It was so good to be with family again. Even if they were extended family and not the ones he was born to.

* * * * *

As kids, Wes and his cousins had started hanging around the local tack shop. Eyeing up the leather tool-work and the latest in lightweight saddles. Back then they didn't have any cash to spend but the owner still tolerated the Roshannon boys being in the way.

Now Wes had grown accustomed to bike shops. The cultures of cowboy and biker were different, but he appreciated both equally. But today, dressed to avoid road rash and with a wad of cash in his pocket from bringing in another fugitive, he felt a kinship to the sleek leather embossed with the insignia of a local chapter of the Bighorns.

He wanted to run his fingers over the arching letters with the jagged triangles representing mountains but had learned enough about club culture that to do without being a member was disrespectful.

"Turned out pretty sick, didn't it?" the shop owner said from beside him.

"It's pretty fucking hot," Wes agreed.

"Custom order. The guy who crafted it poured a metal stamp just for the Bighorns. The piece is going on the wall of their club, I hear. A gift for one of their oldest members."

Today Wes hadn't come in here looking for answers, but his ears perked up. "The club's been around a long time then?"

The shop owner arched a brow at him. "Oh yeah. The Bighorns have been around forever. Split into two chapters, both pretty hidden from outsiders."

The door opened and a rough guy came in looking for a part. It had to be special ordered, so the shop owner circled the counter to do that. Wes roamed the space some more, checking out chaps, jackets and custom saddlebags. But he kept revolving back to that Bighorns piece.

A flat of thick black leather couldn't intrigue him more than a coveted breastplate did to a twelve-year-old ranch boy with dreams of a 4-H win.

The door opened and closed again and suddenly the shop got really small. Six bikers, all wearing the same patches on their leather vests they called cuts. When one turned aside, Wes caught the Bighorns insignia on his back.

He slowed his breathing, aware that his heart was pounding a bit too hard. He'd spent a lot of time researching, visiting and becoming a friend of clubs, so how had this one flown under his radar? The shop owner had said the Bighorns were secretive, but his skills at finding people should be better than that.

All this searching for his mother's history and his true father was throwing him off his game.

While the group spoke with the shop owner and the other customer, Wes neared the group, the club etiquette ingrained in him after a year of hanging around bikers. He stood on the side until a guy noticed him.

The biker fixed him in his stare. Wes stepped up and extended a hand. "Hey man, just wanted to pay my respects. I'm Dirty."

The biker threw his head back and laughed. "I don't want to know how you got that name. I'm James from the Bighorns."

"Good to meet you, James." He gripped his hand and met his gaze.

"Yo, Breaker, this here's Dirty." James tapped the guy next to him on the shoulder.

Breaker turned and fixed Wes in his gaze. "He don't look dirty to me."

Wes grinned and shook his hand. "Breaker." He found repeating the names impressed them in his mind. It was the worst disrespect to forget a name.

The rest of the guys came forward to meet Wes and the ice was broken. Behind the counter, the shop owner eyed Wes with a new gleam of respect in his eyes. It wasn't easy to interact with bikers this way. They stuck to themselves. But Wes had enough experience by this point that he could infiltrate the Hells Angels.

"What're you riding?" James asked him.

Wes told him and added how he'd souped up the engine and tricked out the body. James nodded in appreciation.

Finally, Wes felt comfortable pointing to the leather work he'd been admiring. "That the piece you're here for today?"

James followed his gaze. "Oh yeah. Turned out fucking beautiful, didn't it?" He stroked his graying goatee as he admired it.

"I'd love to support your club. Do you have an event?"

James bobbed his head and reached into an inside pocket of his cut, coming out with a folded flyer. Wes took it and read over the bike night they were throwing as a way to support patients at a nearby VA hospital.

"This is great." He meant it. Most of the clubs he'd hung around supported charities from children to the elderly. Wes admired all their efforts, but he could get behind this cause. His cousin Aiden had been a Marine and he'd met his share of war vets in Operation Freedom Flag.

"You can count on me to be there," he said to James.

The man clapped him on the back. "'Preciate it, man. Look me up."

"I will." He understood he was dismissed and drifted away but kept an ear on their conversation as they were presented with the leather work and paid for it in cash.

Wes waited till they left the shop and the sound of their engines had faded before he leaned on the counter and looked at the owner. "How can I find that club?"

The man eyed him warily. "If you're smart you'll just attend their bike night and not walk up to them on their own turf."

"So they're tougher than most?"

The man narrowed his eyes. "Awful interested, aren't ya?"

"Yeah, I am. I'm new to town and I'm lookin' to find guys who love the life."

"Being stupid could get your ass hurt."

Wes pulled up his sleeve to show a burn mark on his forearm where one of the fugitives he'd been chasing across the county had tried to stub out his cigarette. Next to that was a twisted scar he'd gotten when a horse kicked him, but the guy didn't need to know that.

"I'm no stranger to pain."

The shop owner grunted. "The club's hidden in the foothills. Not easy to find."

"That's all the information I need."

Wes purchased a few items out of courtesy and left. His bike waited for him. He curled his fingers around the handlebars and eased his leg over, mounting it with no less reverence than he would a horse.

He'd come to think of himself as walking between worlds. The cowboy he was at Eagle Crest wasn't the same man who got along with bikers. Yet if he was right about his roots, his father had been—or was—a club guy. His momma had spent time with bikers and come home pregnant. She'd given Wes up to her sister and her new husband to raise.

He could take the shop owner's advice and attend the bike night to ease his way into the Bighorns. But he wasn't the kind of guy who waited around for things to happen. He took action.

He had a reputation for getting things done. People relied on him to get it done. He sure as hell wasn't slacking off in his own affairs, sitting on his thumb waiting.

Heading out of the small town and into the foothills, he steeled himself for what was to come.

* * * * *

As Stormy walked into the clubhouse kitchen, she threw a look at the women sitting around the table, sharing coffee and gossip.

"Now Stormy, sweetie, how the hell do you do that?"

"What are you complaining about now, DeeDee?" Stormy walked to the coffeepot and grabbed a mug. She needed the caffeine to wake up, not get sober after a long night of partying. Though after celebrating Sundance's thirtieth year with the Bighorns, there had been a lot of booze flowing.

"You were awake all night same as we were." DeeDee waved her hand around the table. "But you look like you just stepped out of a spa."

"She's right. Girl, your skin glows," another lady added.

"That's from a hot shower." Stormy scoffed off their compliments. She took her mug to the table and sank into a seat. "What's on the agenda today? Chili to cook?"

"Yeah, we got the big pots out and ready to go. Green Hills chapter riding out tomorrow and we gotta give them a good send-off."

"Where's my dad?" Stormy asked, taking a sip.

"Heard Druid on the phone with your brother," DeeDee said in a lowered voice. The woman was in her late thirties but looked like Stormy's older sister.

Stormy straightened. "My brother?"

"Yeah. I wondered if he was bringing him in for Sundance's party. He's a Bighorn too, after all."

Stormy's brother Alexander had been living outside the club for months now. He'd fallen out with some members and their father, known as Druid, had sent him away. But when Stormy asked him about it, he'd only kiss her softly between the eyes the way daddies kiss their little girls and say, "I'll handle it, okay?"

She pushed out an irritated sigh. "Well, if he's bringing Alexander back, I'll have a chance to talk to him at least. I haven't been able to get hold of him in months."

"Men come and go, girl. Time you get used to that, even if they're your family." DeeDee had been the mother figure Stormy had never known, and the woman was always offering advice. But Stormy'd grown up around the Bighorns and she knew what DeeDee said was true. Nobody could hold these men

17

down for long. There was a reason they chose the Bighorns—and it wasn't only the freedom they got on two wheels.

A scraping noise of chairs being shoved back from tables in the other room had all five ladies in the kitchen on their feet.

A sound like that meant trouble. Stormy started toward the door.

DeeDee grabbed for her sleeve. "Your dad won't be too happy with you walking into men's business."

"I'm not a child and I have a right to know what's going on." She walked out the door.

Behind her, DeeDee said, "That sassy mouth o' hers will be the death of me."

"You're the one who encouraged her to speak her mind at all times," another woman commented.

Stormy entered the main room of the club, hanging with smoke and smelling of last night's party. Liquor and sex.

The guys were all on their feet, as expected, a wall of black leather and rough denim, facing the monitor in the corner of the room. But they weren't watching sports—they were looking at the live surveillance footage.

A lone biker had just rolled up to the club, parked his bike and was walking up as bold as if he was a brother.

Stormy's gaze glued to the screen. The man was tall and built but that was all she could make out.

18

"Dumb fucker, ain't he?" her dad said.

"Doesn't know the code, that's for sure. Time to head this off before he reaches the door," Breaker said.

Three men moved toward the big metal door that wasn't remotely welcoming and anybody who knew the Bighorns realized you couldn't just walk through without invitation from one of the club members.

Stormy held her breath. Her father reached over the bar for a nightstick and caught sight of her. "Get back in the kitchen, Stormy."

She raised her jaw a notch and met his stare. There were other women in the room, and she had just as much right to be here.

A rap on the door had her father turning away, leaving her forgotten. Silence fell over the group.

"Who the fuck is this guy?" someone asked.

"Ballsy, ain't he?"

"No, he's plain stupid," her father snapped.

"I'll go out and ask him what he wants," Stormy offered.

Her father growled, which slapped grins over the faces of several big burly guys who just loved seeing her father go apeshit trying to shield his little girl from the club life he'd introduced her to.

"Stormy." Her name came out as a warning.

But she wasn't listening. She was gawking at the door as it opened.

Two guys rushed it, hurling it open and facing down the man who stood there.

A man dressed in black wasn't so unusual around here. But Stormy held her breath as she got a clear view of the man's face. Angular jaw with a stubborn tilt, a chiseled nose and dark, dark eyes.

What color were they? Brown or black for sure. She grabbed onto a chair to steady herself as she waited for what would come.

"Who the fuck're you?" Her father barked the question.

Breaker threw out an arm across her father's chest. "Wait a minute. James, isn't this the guy we just met at the shop?"

James moved through the group to the door, not looking very happy with what he saw. He folded his arms over his chest and eyed the newcomer. "You got a problem understanding the protocol here?"

"I mean no disrespect."

"Opening a door that doesn't belong to you's a damn good sign of disrespect," her father said.

"Let me handle this. The guy seemed fine at the shop." James stepped outside with him and closed the door. On the screen, Stormy watched the back of James's head blocking her view of the guest.

Her father glared at her from across the room, but she'd long ago learned to stand up to him. He might be the protective father in all the right ways but at times it got out of hand.

Ignoring him, she watched the screen. James turned to the door and came inside, leaving the newcomer outside. He didn't leave, though, just stood waiting, looking as if he owned the place.

"He's asking for Sundance."

"He asked for him by name?" Her father looked surprised.

"He asked for the member who's been here longest. Says Sundance knew his mother."

"Stormy, go get Sundance."

Chapter Two

Wes Roshannon went balls to the wall and never said die. But he'd basically stomped on all the rules by demanding entrance to the Bighorns' club. These guys weren't going to open their door like Grandma for the Big Bad Wolf, but he'd lost his mind a little thinking that the man who'd fathered him could be inside.

The club perched on the side of the foothill surrounded by pines like an ornament on a Christmas tree. The low building was large enough to house a lot of chickens or sheep. But Wes wasn't in ranchin' country anymore.

Inside were a lot of rough men, some he'd probably seen on the walls of the fugitive recovery office he was dispatched from. But he wasn't here for that reason.

He stared at the metal door, waiting for the verdict. Things could go wrong fast, though he was confident he could handle pretty much anything.

Finally, James came out again and closed the door.

"You're lucky, Dirty. We've got some guys inside who'd like to use you for target practice, but I vouched for your good behavior. Don't make me look bad."

Wes nodded. "Thank you."

James's expression was far from welcoming as he opened the door and stepped inside. Wes followed.

The interior was dimly-lit and clouded with smoke, and he couldn't make out the shapes of people right away. But as soon as he stepped inside and someone else shut the door behind him, his eyes adjusted.

A dozen or so men stood like guards with hands on hips or folded over their chests. Wes resisted the urge to reach for his sidearm. Knowing he couldn't risk insulting these guys by bringing a weapon onto their turf, he'd left it in his saddlebag. He couldn't risk challenging them either. But in a pinch, he didn't need firepower when a perfectly good knife was stuffed down his boot, and Wes had taken on worse situations.

"Who the fuck're you? And why are you looking for Sundance?" A brute of a man stepped up to Wes. Dark hair with strands of white running through it gave away his age as late forties. He was as big as Wes but lacking the bulk he had and he bore a jagged scar through one eyebrow, splitting it in two.

"He knew my mother," Wes answered. "Her name was Blanche. Went by Baby?"

A wiry-looking man with steel-gray long hair and piercing blue eyes moved into the greenish light cast from overhead.

Wes went still. This had to be Sundance.

He studied the man. Okay, studied was an understatement. He drank in his appearance like a shipwrecked man slurped up water. But what he saw wasn't quenching his thirst.

Wes was six-two and two hundred pounds with thick dark hair and steel gray eyes. But Sundance—the only man who might be his real, unnamed father—stood much shorter with a toughness to his smaller frame like dried meat clinging to the bone. His hair was faded to gray, but Wes could tell by the lack of pepper amidst the salt that Sundance had never had dark hair.

And their eyes were completely different, though Sundance could give a hell of a mean glower.

He peered at Wes more closely. "Known lots of women over the years. Who was your mother again?"

"Blanche Washington."

Sundance's gaze zeroed in on him.

"I think she was called Baby."

Sundance blinked. "Now that's a blast from the past. Hell yeah. I knew your momma, boy. Jesus Christ, you're a big 'un. I never would have guessed she'd have a son of your size. Sit and have a beer with me."

Wes's pulse jumped as he realized this was it—he'd tracked down the right guy who could tell him more about the woman who'd birthed him, then run out, leaving Wes with her sister and brother-in-law to raise him.

The place smelled of booze and something earthier that was weed or sex or both.

Sundance nodded toward the wooden row of stools in front of a bar and circled behind. "Pull up a stool. What do they call you?"

"Dirty."

"Now that's a memorable name. Who gave it to ya?" Sundance grabbed four beers, two in each hand. He set them on the bar, and Wes realized no one else was drinking with them. They each had two.

He sank to a stool and wrapped his fingers around the cold beer to steady himself. This was fucking surreal, coming here. How many years had he thought about doing just this?

Since he was a kid, wondering why the cousins he shared a home with had a mom and dad and he didn't.

Or since he was eight years old and rumors started flying that his real daddy was actually the man he lived with, his uncle Matthias Roshannon. A lawman had to investigate every lead before coming to a conclusion, though, and Wes was touching all his bases with the biker club.

"I was in Colorado for a while and the Disciples gave me the nickname."

Sundance grunted at the mention of the other club, and Wes went on. "Funny story. I was invited up to the clubhouse for a barbecue and it was raining when I set out. By the time I reached the club, I was soaked to the skin and covered with road muck."

A woman edged up to the end of the bar. Wes turned his head and met her stare. Warm brown eyes and long dark hair along with a peaches and cream complexion made him forget what he was saying.

Then the big man who'd challenged him at the door stepped in front of her, blocking her from Wes's view. He took her by the arm and led her out of the room.

Wes swung his attention back to Sundance, hoping he hadn't committed another social crime. He'd probably find his ass beaten and tossed out after what he'd pulled to get inside.

Sundance didn't sit but remained behind the bar, steadily watching him. Wes had a hell of a poker face, though, and the man wouldn't see anything to raise suspicions. Lifting his beer to Wes, Sundance said, "Let's drink to your momma."

"To Blanche."

"To Baby."

They clinked bottles and Wes pursed his lips around the bottle. The hops and flavors hit his tongue, a welcome distraction from the fire coursing through his system. His mind was still on that woman. The way she'd fixed her gaze on him, so boldly…

Sundance drained his beer and turned his bloodshot, wary stare on Wes.

He nursed his own beer, weighing his words. And he eyed Sundance's empty bottle. All he needed was a split second of distraction to gather the DNA off the rim. "So you knew my mother."

He nodded. "That I did. Beautiful woman, couldn't find a sweeter one. Thought she'd make a fine old lady to someone one day if… Well, I was sorry for what happened."

Sorry that she'd overdosed on sleeping pills and never lived long enough for her son to confront her about giving him up.

Wes nodded his acceptance. The other members had relaxed a fraction, no longer surrounding him as if ready to pick him up and spear him on a spit. But they were still watching him — closely.

Sundance talked about his mother for a while, giving Wes the stories about her time here with the Bighorns that he'd longed for his entire life. Out of the corner of his eye, he spotted the dark-haired beauty again. She stood off to the side and he noted that when the big guy moved, she did too. Trying to keep out of his sight?

Finally, the oldest member and leader of the club asked Wes what he was riding. They went outside to look at his bike along with a few other guys acting as guard in case Wes pulled any shit.

"You're a Harley man. Your momma would approve."

"Can't resist beautiful curves on a bike or a woman, can we?"

Sundance barked a laugh. "No, that we can't."

Wes touched his pocket, hoping the film with the smear of DNA would be enough.

Then Sundance clapped a hand on Wes's shoulder. He didn't realize it was a dismissal until the man pointed to the road leading down into town. "A clear ride home for you. C'mon back and see us, Dirty. Baby was a dear friend of mine, and I see her strength and her love of life in your eyes."

All the way back home, Wes played and replayed this encounter. The lawman side of his mind tried to pinpoint some action that would cause him to question Sundance—his motives, what was truth or falsity. But he couldn't find any holes in what Sundance had shared with him.

Wes had to get the DNA analyzed, but his guess was Sundance was as much his father as Donald Trump. He was no further in his search than when he'd begun.

It shouldn't matter so damn much, should it? He'd been raised well, as one of the Roshannons. His cousins Judd and Aiden were like his brothers. His aunt couldn't have treated him more like a son. And

Uncle Matthias... well, he was a hard rancher who didn't show much emotion, but he was always good to Wes.

His mind wandered back to the Bighorns and the way the gorgeous woman had flashed a look at him that in any other situation, would have had him on his feet, talking to her.

She was probably about the same age his mother had been while here. Young, full of life and promise, and possessing a beauty that would lure in any man with a pair of eyes and a cock.

The road stretched before him. Where it would take him now, he had no friggin' idea.

But there were always fugitives to hunt. For now, it had to be enough.

* * * * *

Stormy sat at the computer, working on the next event flyer for the club. There was always something going on, and she welcomed the work.

The Bighorns had to look like a nonprofit, but that wasn't too difficult. They were always holding some fundraiser. She did the bookkeeping, recording where every dime went. From buying gas cards for guys who had to travel back and forth to the VA hospital for chemo to someone who couldn't make his mortgage payment.

These things made Stormy proud to be part of the club. It was the other shit that went on — the stuff her father didn't want her knowing—that had her questioning what a life away from the bikers would be like.

She had an itchy feeling that Alexander was involved in the dirtier goings-on and that was the reason he'd been sent away.

Dirtier.

Dirty.

That man had some guts coming to the club that way. She couldn't help but admire his strength and determination to get info about his momma. Family meant a lot to Stormy, and his mission was admirable.

Who was she kidding? She liked the way he looked.

As big as her daddy but thickly muscled, his shoulders so huge that a woman could shelter beneath them. And those eyes. They'd been dark all right—steel gray, nearly black. And the way he'd looked at her...

She wrapped her arms around her middle, holding in those quivery feelings she hadn't felt in too long. With her father around and only the same old biker family to look at day in and day out, she didn't have any romantic opportunities. She was protected from the worst of the world, which she could appreciate. But when she thought of what she wanted out of life, she couldn't picture herself here with a Bighorn, having his babies and looking after him forever.

She loved the club—the members were her family, but there was something else out there for her.

She leaned back in her chair to examine the flyer she'd made. The raffle tickets would be sold for $100 each and the winner received the latest model motorcycle. Happy with her work, she sent the document to the printer.

When the sheet flew off the printer, she plucked it up and walked out of the small room serving as her office. All events had to be approved through Sundance, and where he'd be at this time of day was anybody's guess.

Popping her head into the kitchen, she saw DeeDee wiping down counters. The woman was a permanent fixture here, a mother to all, the best of friends to her and so many other women who lived or passed through the club.

DeeDee looked up from cleaning. "What's up, pretty?"

"You seen Sundance?"

"Garage."

Stormy threw her a cross-eyed look, which had DeeDee chuckling, and breezed out, flyer in hand.

She didn't take two steps out the front door when she set eyes on *him*. Dirty.

God, the man lived up to that name. Her mind exploded with at least twenty dirty thoughts about him and what she could do to him. That big, muscled body would be good for taking for a ride.

She bit her lower lip, wondering if she could approach him without her father's radar going off and him running interference. Dirty stood near his bike. It gleamed in the sun like a beacon.

Without thought, she moved toward him.

At her approach, he glanced her way. Then angled his body to face her. The way he hooked his thumb in his jeans pocket sent a shiver through her.

As she closed the gap between them, her insides heated. Just seeing the man up close did things to her body she had no idea happened between a man and woman. The couples who hooked up at the club seemed to do so less out of chemistry and more out of raw need. And she was never part of that. Even if she wanted to, her daddy wouldn't allow anyone near her.

"Hey." Dirty's voice was deep, gritty and melted a woman's ovaries. She felt them throb with the primal need to have a man like him. Strong, tough and fucking hot as hell.

When their gazes locked, she forgot how to speak.

"I saw you the other day. What's your name?" A hint of a smile toyed around the corner of his lips as if he knew exactly what effect he had on her. He probably saw it all the time with women. Hell, even men.

"Stormy."

He grinned. "Fits you."

She eyed him. "What's that supposed to mean?"

"You look like the kind of woman who can upset the universe."

She didn't know whether to be flattered or insulted. The way Dirty was looking at her, though, had her leaning toward the compliment.

He did that sexy chin nod thing a lot of Bighorns did. But from him, it was... so... much... hotter. "What's that in your hand?"

She remembered the flyer she still clutched. "Oh. It's a new event." She held it out for him to read and he nodded.

"I'll be there to support the cause. Can I get a ticket now?"

"Oh. Not yet. I need to run this by Sundance first." She should ask where the president of the club was, but she didn't want to quit talking to Dirty.

"Okay, well, I'll find you to buy a ticket when I'm able to."

Hot stuff, you can find me for any reason at all.

She let her gaze roam over his rugged features. Tanned skin and small creases around each eye from squinting into the sun as he navigated all that power between his legs.

She squeezed her thighs together and he dipped his gaze over her body. Her stomach dropped along with it.

"So Stormy, what do you do outside the club?"

She blinked. "I, um, spend most of my time here."

His expression darkened. "Are you with one of the guys?"

"Oh. No, Druid's my dad."

Dirty swung his gaze to the garage where all the guys were most likely congregated, talking club business, which was why Dirty wasn't allowed in. He wasn't a member. "Druid's your father?"

She nodded.

"Damn," he said quietly.

The sound of the curse shouldn't make her nipples harden, but it did.

Dirty landed his stare on her, pinning her firmly. "You wanna get out of here for a while?"

Her jaw dropped. "Take a ride? With you?"

He nodded. "What do you say?"

Her father would kill her. No, he'd kill Dirty. But she could talk sense to him before he broke both of Dirty's legs. And the opportunity was too good.

She dropped the flyer and reached for his helmet dangling off the handlebar.

He flashed her a grin and arched a brow as if tempting her to do more than try his helmet on for size. He slipped his leg over the bike and flipped the kickstand. She fastened the helmet and climbed on behind him, arms around his thick middle and thighs braced around his muscled hips.

He threw her a look over his shoulder that made her ovaries finally explode. "Hold on, baby."

She was in deep shit, and not only because her father was going to kill Dirty and lock her in her room. But oh yeah, it was worth it.

* * * * *

Having a woman's arms around him and her legs locked tight onto his thighs as Wes took the curves heading out of the foothills was the reason men loved bikes, he was convinced. He was far too aware he had precious cargo on board, and not only because of who Stormy's father was to the Bighorns.

Wes would sooner destroy a champion stallion than let any harm come to her.

She fit against him like a piece of a puzzle. Her soft breasts plastered to his back, her parted thighs —

He couldn't think on it long. She already had his balls aching and bluer than the Wyoming sky.

"Faster," she said into his ear.

A thrill hit his stomach that had little to do with the heat of her breath on his skin. She liked it fast, just as he did. He didn't know much about this woman, but he was damn well going to find out more — whether her father approved or not.

He was already on the guy's radar for looking at Stormy. Once Druid discovered he'd taken her on the back of his bike, he'd better have his wits about him and be prepared to duck Druid's fists.

Right now, with the open road stretching before them and a beautiful woman with her thighs spread for him, he didn't give a damn what he'd be facing once he returned her to the club. He couldn't even pretend he hadn't returned to the Bighorns to see more of her. Something about her pulled at him.

Fresh air scented with pine and growing things was spiced with a deeper hint of woman. Sweet, delicious woman. He had no doubt that if he pulled her hair aside and buried his nose against her throat that he'd find more reasons to stick around the club.

He planned on doing both.

Keeping his eyes peeled for a pull-off, he noted the way she adjusted herself to his every movement. Just as she'd done with her father to hide from him, but she seemed to be trying to get closer to Wes.

When he spied the grassy area off the road, he throttled down and eased to a stop. She leaned closer, shooting pangs of pure desire to his cock.

"What are we doing?" she asked.

"I thought we could talk."

She nodded and moved. He felt her arms stretch upward so she could remove the helmet. Then her long hair brushed his arm.

He wanted to get off the bike and talk face to face, but it was a bad idea. He wasn't the type of guy to hold back when he wanted something, and Stormy roused his deeper instincts.

He twisted his neck to look at her over his shoulder. "What do you do around the club?"

"Well, I work with the ladies, making sure everyone's fed and comfortable. And I'm sort of a Sundance's personal assistant."

Wes felt a flip of jealousy and bit back a growl. The word personal better not mean what he thought it did.

"You're not with anyone, right? Nobody's going to come after me for putting you on my bike, are they?"

"You didn't 'put me' on your bike. I climbed on myself. And no, I'm nobody's old lady."

Silence filled his ears as he just took in the moment. She leaned forward to look at his face and they shared a look that got his cock fully hard. One flash of her eyes and he was a goner—he couldn't be responsible for carrying her to a spot of shade and having his way with her.

Trouble was, once he claimed her, he wouldn't give her up. He didn't think she was prepared for that.

"What do you do when you're not hanging around bike clubs, Dirty?"

He felt the words on his tongue and didn't hold back from speaking. "I grew up on a ranch an hour or so from here."

"Horses?" She sounded like an excited girl.

He nodded. "My uncle's got a big herd of Angus too."

She whistled. "That's worth some bucks."

"He does well. I go there as often as I can to help him. You mentioned horses. Do you ride?"

"I haven't since I was a kid, but I used to love it."

"Then I'll take you there."

She looked at him, her lips inches away. He could kiss her but then he'd never stop.

"I'd like that, Dirty," she said almost breathlessly.

At the sound of a motorcycle engine—no, *engines*—she stiffened against him. "They're coming for me."

"It's more likely they're coming for *me*," he responded and set wheels to the road again, going more slowly this time so the Bighorns could catch up. They surrounded them, with Druid riding right alongside, giving Dirty a look that could kill a lesser man. But Dirty wasn't backing down from this guy's intimidation tactics. There was far too much chemistry between him and Stormy to give up to an angry papa.

With a dozen bikers circling him, he had no choice but to head their direction back to the club. After he pulled in and cut the engine, Druid barked at Stormy. "Get off that bike."

"Dad, don't treat me like a child. We just went for a ride."

The man dismounted from his ride and crossed to where Wes was parked, fists clenched. He didn't look at his daughter when he spoke but glared at Wes.

"I said get off that bike, Stormy."

"Not if you're going to give Dirty trouble." She tightened her hold on him.

Wes had to defuse the situation. He rested a hand over hers where it clung to his middle. "It's okay, Stormy."

"Don't fucking talk to her like she belongs to you," Druid bit off.

Wes swung his leg over his bike and stood to face the man. "She doesn't belong to anyone, far as I see. She made the choice to come with me and I've returned her safe."

"Without my permission," Druid growled, getting in Wes's face.

Damn, what he wouldn't give to lay hands on the man right now. Wes hated being challenged — it went back to his days of being bullied as a skinny, weak kid. He ground his molars and stared Druid down.

"If you're smart you'll drive out of here while you still have the use of all your limbs." Druid's threat raised a gasp from Stormy.

She grabbed her father's arm and tried to pull him away. "Stop it. It was just a ride."

"It's okay, Stormy." Wes swung his gaze to her and fuck, the way she looked at him... All rosy cheeks and plump, bitten lips he hadn't even gotten a chance to kiss. This wouldn't be the last she'd see of him. He tried to convey the message in the look they exchanged before getting back on his bike.

He'd hunt some fugitives while giving Druid time to cool off—the other Bighorns too. But he sure as hell wasn't giving up that easy, not when he hadn't felt this good in far too long.

Chapter Three

Wes raised a hand and rapped his knuckles on the door of the small house needing major repairs. Hanging out in a dump like this wasn't Van Atkin's style. The fugitive was originally wanted on charges of a petty theft for shoplifting DVDs. Since jumping bail, he'd made stealing a part-time job. And evading Wes a full-time one.

A scuff of a step behind the door had him tensing, on red alert. Van Atkins had fled from him several times — gotten away every damn time too. He was starting to piss Wes off.

The door opened a crack and he peered at the face framed here. A woman, looking wary of life itself and not just Wes's presence.

"Who're you?" she asked in a drawl that was too Southern to be a Wyoming woman.

"Old friend of Van's. He home?"

She gripped the door harder. "What makes you think he lives here?"

"Heard from a buddy o' his by the name of Wilder that he's here." Wes shrugged, conjuring his inner actor. He'd learned acting like a buddy with the person's best interests in mind got him further than marching in, threatening them with the full weight of the law. He acted like their friend, like he was doing them a favor by helping them get before the judge. And he told those harboring the criminals that he wanted the best for them.

Of course, he did. He wasn't ruthless, but he was far from soft.

"You talked to Jack?" the woman asked.

"Yeah, though he said his foot's been paining him. Guess he broke it a few months back?"

She nodded absently, eyes cutting to the side.

Wes could shove the door open and probably see his bounty standing there, instructing her about what to do or say.

He refrained.

"Can I come in, ma'am?" He tugged on his Stetson.

Her eyes narrowed. Yeah, she was definitely concealing Atkins from him.

"No, you can't. Van's not here. So I'd ask you kindly to leave."

"Doesn't sound so kindly to me," Wes responded.

She moved to shut the door, and he planted a hand on it to keep that from happening. He pushed. She pushed back.

"Ma'am, this isn't about you. I have a deal with Van that if he goes before the judge for his hearing that he won't end up in jail for that particular crime."

A smashing sound came from within, and Wes shoved the door inward in time to see his fugitive racing out a back door.

Wes whirled and ran. Leaping off the dumpy porch steps and hitting the ground at top speed. A big guy like him wasn't a track star, but he was fast. He gained on his quarry. "Van! Stop right there!"

The guy ran willy-nilly, as Aunt Winter liked to call it, zigzagging through his neighbor's yards, trying to throw off Wes.

A car screeched up on the street, the door flung open. Van dived into the open door and they peeled away, the woman at the wheel.

"Dammit." Wes ripped off his hat and shoved his fingers through his hair. His heart was pumping hard but not from the run. He was pissed at himself for losing the guy again. His boss wasn't going to like hearing it any better than Wes would like saying it.

He walked back to his truck parked some distance down the street and made the call. Got his ass chewed. His boss asked why the best bounty hunter this side of the Mississippi wasn't able to bring in a simple shoplifter. But Wes had no excuses and didn't offer any.

Finally, he started the engine and drove toward the town where Judd lived and worked as sheriff. As he navigated the country roads, he should be thinking up ways to finally nab his bounty, but his mind was back with the Bighorns... and Stormy.

The memory of the gorgeous woman clinging to him wasn't something he'd soon forget, if ever. Her perfume seemed to linger on in his nose and it had been over a week since they'd been together.

By the time Wes walked into the sheriff's office, his agitation came out in the form of a growl.

"Birdie. Where's Judd."

The woman sat behind the front desk, eyes glued to the computer screen. But at Wes's less-than-friendly tone, she peered over the top of the unit with her best look reserved for the Roshannon boys.

"Sorry," he muttered. "Do you know where Judd is?"

"Of course I do. It's my job to know where the sheriff and deputies are at all times." Her well-duh tone didn't help Wes feel any better.

"Okay, so will you tell me where he is?" When she didn't blink once at him, he added, "Please?" Damn, Judd's office worker was a ball-buster.

At last, he got a smile from the woman. "Why, he's down the road at the diner grabbing some takeout. I told him to sit there and have a meal, but he's ornery as a coon in a garbage can. Once his mind's fixed on something, there's no changing it."

Wes chuckled. "About sums up Judd. I'll head down and catch him."

Two minutes later, he spotted the familiar battered Stetson across the diner and angled for him. Judd stood as tall as he did, but Wes had spent years bulking up. In his line of work, you could never be too big. Stopping criminals wasn't easy work—almost nobody came quietly.

Judd glimpsed him as he approached, and a smile spread over his face. "Cuz. What brings you to this neck of the woods? Hunting a new bounty? That dumbass Erikson is stupid enough to jump bail."

He shook his head, meeting eyes the same hue of his own. "Nah, never seen anyone named Erikson come through the dispatch. I was looking into the matter I put on your desk last time I was in town."

Judd pressed his lips together and gave a nod. At that moment, the waitress who didn't look old enough to be out of high school passed a brown bag across the counter to Judd.

"Shouldn't she be in school?" he asked Judd.

"Tell me about it. They're looking young and younger."

"Or we're older."

"Speak for yourself," his cousin joked.

Wes snorted. "Do you want to sit and eat?"

"Hell, no. I can't even find my desk. I'll probably have to hold this container on my lap while I eat and work at the same time. Do you want anything?"

"Nah, grabbed a burger on the way."

"Good. C'mon."

In the parking lot, Judd waved for Wes to join him in his truck, but Wes stopped short of getting in.

45

"Look, I just need to know the results of the DNA I gave ya. I have to get back to work."

Judd cocked a brow at him. "Atkins again?"

"Yeah. Motherfucker ran from me before I came up here."

"Either you need to get a sidekick or find a new way to corner him." Judd shook his head.

"Yeah, I've never had so much trouble before. Not even from guys with much darker, more violent pasts." Hell, he'd run terrorist groups to the ground easier in his days working for the government.

"Okay, but are you sure you wanna hear it in the parking lot?" Judd glanced around at the beat-up trucks and late-model SUVs with four-wheel-drive the people needed to traverse the mountain roads of Wyoming.

Wes dipped his head in a harsh nod. "I can handle whatever you have to tell me."

Judd opened the door of his SUV and placed the food bag on his seat. Then he closed the door and leaned against the vehicle.

Fuck, this couldn't be good news.

"Out with it."

"That DNA doesn't match yours, Wes."

A sigh trickled out of him, but it didn't take him more than a few heartbeats to recover. "That's what I thought."

"What the hell are you doin', anyway? Lookin' for a brother?"

"Sorta."

"You can't just drop shit like this in my lap without an explanation."

"It's not a match. Nothing more to say. Thanks for running the labs, Judd. 'Preciate it." With that, he started back toward his truck.

"Hold up. You coming to Eagle Crest anytime soon?"

"Hope to meet there next weekend, but it depends on what gets done between now and then."

"Same here. My workload's insane and I've been ignoring my wife. See ya when I see ya. Stay safe, Wes."

He tipped his hat to his cousin and got behind the wheel. He waited a long minute for his heart to slow before pulling out, just breathing.

Sundance was not his father. He'd known it. But on many fronts, the information wasn't a bit of comfort. Because now it meant there was only one other path to take.

And he wasn't prepared for the outcome. Not yet.

He drove all the way back to his office and gave his report about Atkins. A few more fines were dropped on the man's head and Wes was given new leads as to where he could find the guy.

He stared at the sheaf of wanted photos his boss handed him. Wes flipped through the papers. "I'll take care of these the next few days and then I'm taking a week off. I have some business to see to."

Such as driving back up that mountain to the biker club. Since leaving, every cell in him had been burning to see Stormy again.

His boss clapped him on the back. "Do what you do. I know you'll get it done."

Oh yeah, if he found Stormy within a mile of that club, he'd get it done, all right. Hard and thoroughly too.

He smiled genuinely for the first time that day.

* * * * *

Stormy lay on a sofa, one bare leg dangling off. Her shorts too short for her daddy's tastes and her top riding up. But he wasn't here. Nobody was except a few club girls.

The TV was on, volume low, but she wasn't watching it. She was daydreaming about a big blue sky and taking the curves with her arms around a beautiful, muscled man.

She'd spent all of half an hour with Dirty and she hadn't stopped thinking of him in more than a week. She'd heard DeeDee talk about Sam and wondered how she felt such emotions for him. She used words like love at first sight and love of a lifetime. Stormy hadn't understood at all.

Until she'd met Dirty.

Maybe she was acting like a smitten schoolgirl, but there was an unspoken connection between them. And in those minutes alone with him on his bike, she'd experienced more living than she had in all her twenty-four years.

Suddenly, DeeDee walked in and stopped.

Stormy focused on her though all she saw in her mind's eye was the big biker with steely-gray eyes. "What is it, DeeDee? Do you need help with something?"

The thin woman came into the space to lean against the arm of the sofa where Stormy lay.

She pushed onto her elbows. "What's wrong?"

"I don't know if I should be doing this or not," DeeDee said.

Stormy sat up, tugging her top down over her midriff. "Spit it out, DeeDee."

"Someone's here."

She was on her feet in a blink. She walked out into the main room. Across the sea of tables and chairs, she met Dirty's warm, heavy gaze.

The corner of his lips tipped upward, all for her.

"Hey, you." He took a step.

She did too.

"I shouldn't be here with all the Bighorns gone, but I couldn't go away without seeing you."

She wove through the tables to stand before him. "Don't go."

49

His throat worked on a hard swallow and he nodded. "Okay, so do we need a chaperone of some kind? That woman who let me in?"

"That's DeeDee, but no. I don't need a chaperone." She caught him by the hand and towed him back outside. The club door slammed shut behind them.

She paused to look up at him, head tilted back and her hair ticklish against her waist where her top had ridden up again. "I'm so glad to see you."

He squeezed her fingers, his warm and callused, probably from that ranch work he'd mentioned.

He gave a small shake of his head that made her look closer at him. "What is it?" she asked.

"I have no idea how you're more beautiful than I remembered because I thought my imagination was pretty damn wild."

A pleasured sigh left her. "You're different, Dirty."

"I'm a man like any other."

"But nobody else makes my heart beat this fast." She took his hand and boldly placed it over her breast where her heart pounded.

He curled his fingers against her and closed his eyes for a brief second. When he opened them, the steel gray depths burned with a need that echoed through her own body. Crazy or not, she wanted him.

"Dirty..."

He moved his hand from her chest to cup her face. His long fingers extending to her temple and the heel of his hand cradling her jaw. She felt the power within him but knew he'd never harm her.

"Tell your dad I'm sorry," he grated out.

"For what?"

"For this." He swooped in and captured her mouth. His lips hard and demanding, his masculine scent of grasses and musk with a hint of leather making her head spin.

A moan left her as she went on tiptoe and kissed him back. Right in front of the door of the club in full view of any Bighorn who drove in.

She didn't give a damn. What she'd known her entire life and what she wanted for herself were at war, and the part of her seeking something of her own won.

She braced her hands on Dirty's broad chest and went on tiptoe to kiss him back. He traced his tongue back and forth over her lips until she parted for him. Then he snaked his tongue against hers with a primal growl.

"Fuck," he groaned between deep passes of his tongue. He planted a hand on her spine and pulled her against him, and her body knew exactly how to mold to fit him. She was made for it.

"I can't stop," he gritted out.

"Then don't. No one's inside and my room has a lock."

He withdrew, staring down at her, chest heaving. "I can't, baby. Fuck, I want to."

She wasn't taking any of his chivalrous restraint bullshit. She grabbed his hand and reached for the door. Tugging the big man through the silent club had her adrenaline rushing. For a second, she wondered if the thrill of being a bad girl and going against her father's wishes wasn't part of her wanting Dirty.

But when they reached her room and he lifted her into his arms with a low, animalistic sound, she knew that wasn't the case.

She wanted him. Now.

* * * * *

He'd spent weeks thinking of little else but the woman. Hell, he'd even dreamed of her, waking to find his cock stiff and throbbing with the echoes of her soft body lingering in his mind.

Now she was kissing the hell out of him, and damn was she good at it. He thrust his tongue into her mouth, drawing a rough moan from her lips. He fed a growl back to her.

"I fucking want you. But if you don't feel the same, say so now."

She pulled back to blink at him. Her eyes... fuck, they carried a mysterious light like a candle luring a man through a dark night to a safe haven.

"Why wouldn't I feel the same? Lay me down on that bed and have your way with me, Dirty. Right now."

He kicked the door shut and twisted the lock. Then he grinned at her demand. Hell, the tables were turned here. In the past, he'd always been the one giving commands, but he didn't want any of his old tricks with this woman. She seemed too fresh, brand-new, for him to don that old hat.

He moved to the bed and set her down. Before she could even bounce on the mattress, he covered her with his body, weighting her thighs under his, her hands pinned overhead by his own.

Staring down at her shouldn't give him that odd fluttering sensation in his chest, but it did. Un-de-fucking-niably.

"You're fucking beautiful. I've wanted you since the first time I saw you."

Her lips popped open on his rough words, giving him a glimpse of her wet, pink tongue. Fuck, what he wanted to do to that tongue. The places he wanted to put it.

"Really?" she whispered.

He nodded. "These curves." He slid his hands over her side, from the round of her breast to the indentation of her waist and down to her flaring hip. "But really it's your eyes that draw me in."

Now he'd gone and said something sappy and corny. She was a woman who lived among bikers—she'd think him ridiculous.

But she didn't laugh. Her gaze burned up at him. "I want you too, Dirty." Her touch on his jaw was brief and then she ran her hand down his neck to his shoulder. When she eased off his leather cut, he watched emotions play over her face.

Lust, longing. Excitement. And something he couldn't put his finger on, even after years of training himself to read faces.

He kissed her again, claiming her mouth in a way that had them both gasping and half-naked by the time the kiss ended. Passion spread through his limbs as he hovered over her, touching her exposed skin for the first time.

Collarbones and the swell of her breasts. He dipped his tongue into her cleavage, tasting a sweetness that dizzied him. When he lifted his head, her eyes were glowing with need.

"Take me. Don't make me wait anymore."

He tore off her clothes, tossing aside her top that refused to stay in place, cutoff denim shorts and tiny panties. When she was completely naked and he was able to get a good long look at her, he dragged in a harsh breath.

"I don't want to hurt you."

"Why would you hurt me?"

"I'm big."

She offered a quirk of her lips. "I'm not going to break, Dirty." She skimmed her hands over his bulge, following the lines of his cock from base to tip, arcing in his jeans. "Mmm, you *are* big. Let me see."

He stood at the side of the bed to unfasten his jeans and kick off his boots. When he reached into the V of his fly and pulled his cock free, she wet her lips.

She ran her tongue right over that plump lower lip in a way he'd carry with him all the way to his grave. She was fucking perfection.

She skimmed her hands over her breasts. "I want to taste you."

He gave a rough shake of his head. "Not now. Because I'm going to taste you."

Starting at her lips, he nibbled his way down her body, giving special attention to her nipples and the flat of her stomach before reaching the soft tuft of curls between her legs. Her rich scents had his cock at full mast and aching like never before. The tip leaked pre-come in a steady stream. All he wanted was to bury himself between her lush thighs and find ecstasy.

When he sank his tongue between her ripe pussy folds, he issued a groan and she answered with a throaty cry. Need spread through him as he explored her, but it didn't take him long to find what she liked.

Her clit hard on his tongue, he alternated between drawing circles around it and pressing it into her body. She fisted his hair, dragging him where she wanted as her ass lifted off the bed and she ground against his mouth.

"Oh God… Your mouth's so good. I'm so close. Make me come, Dirty. Make me…" She broke off on a rasp as shudders vibrated his tongue and juices squeezed from her folds.

He shot upward, his balls ready to burst. He couldn't take more time or it would all be over. As he searched his jeans for a condom and finally located one, he squeezed his fist around the head of his cock, staving off his impending release.

Stormy lay on the bed, beautifully disheveled and pink from her orgasm. Her knees modestly together and her eyes full of hazy desire. "Hurry." Her whisper sent him reeling.

In one swift jerk of his hand, the condom was in place. He nudged her thighs apart and poised at the quick of her.

She used her heels against his ass to drag him into her. The minute his cock was buried deep in her hot, tight pussy, he lost his freakin' mind. Couldn't stop the movement. He pulled out, slammed back in.

She clung to him, her lips roaming over his as he claimed her well and fully.

The tight clutch of her pussy around his cock was the stuff dreams were made of, and he gave himself up to sensation. Her soft body under his hands, her scents on his face and her flavors on his tongue as he thrust into her again and again.

Easing his hands under her ass, he drew her up to receive his plunges. She threw her head back, trembling. On the verge, he realized.

Hold out. Hold the fuck out, Roshannon. His command barely did the trick.

The instant her pussy squeezed him so tight with her release, he was pouring his load into her, hips pumping, an oath muttered.

"Fuck yeah. Fuck, baby. Fucking coming."

What he should have said was, *I'm a fucking goner.*

* * * * *

When the Bighorns returned, Stormy was clothed and seated at a respectful distance from Dirty with DeeDee not far off. But when the guys filed into the room and spotted Dirty, she felt their disapproving stares on her, making her neck hot.

Or maybe Dirty's rough five o'clock shadow had burned her skin when he'd kissed every inch of her neck, down her spine to her buttocks.

Her body clenched at the memory of their encounter. If it never happened again, she would hold it close to her heart as one of the best moments of her life.

He stood as the guys entered the room, between cutting glares his way and worried looks hers. DeeDee got up to embrace her man. He said something in her ear and she nodded. Then she slid her gaze to Stormy.

She held her breath as the last guy entered the room and took note of the man who was not a member of the Bighorns and his only daughter sitting in the same room.

"That's it. Outside." Her dad twitched his head to the door for Dirty to follow.

"No. Dad, what are you doing?" She got up and rushed to him, praying she didn't smell as much like Dirty and sex as she thought she did.

Dirty came up behind her and placed a hand on her shoulder. "It's okay, Stormy."

"Get your hand off her."

The three of them made it outside and DeeDee and Sam followed. Stormy was grateful they had her back. She had no idea how to make her father see she wasn't a kid and his behavior was uncalled for. Dirty was a good man, as good as any Bighorn who came to this club.

But that was the problem — her dad would never let her have any relationship with anyone in or out of the Bighorns. He'd taken his protective act through her teen years right into adulthood. He didn't see her for what she was, and right now she was a woman half in love. Who wanted to hop on the back of Dirty's bike and have him show her a bigger world than what she had right here.

Her father squared up against the man who'd just thoroughly and very satisfyingly loved her. She attempted to move between them but her father gently set her aside.

"Stormy, stay out of this."

"How can I when it's about me? You don't want Dirty around me because you know I like him."

Dirty jerked his gaze to her. Her heart throbbed at what she saw there and prayed her father didn't see it too. Dirty wanted her as much as she wanted him, and anybody with eyes could tell. DeeDee had known it from day one and there was no stopping the momentum now that they'd touched each other.

Her body still hummed from the pleasure he'd given her and she could taste his body on her lips.

"Fuck. I knew I couldn't trust you. Should have killed you after you took my daughter on a ride without my permission."

"Sir, I'd like to get on your good side in this matter." Dirty glanced to the side where two Bighorns had just pulled in with a truck. They got out and carried a duffle bag past the group in front of the door.

Stormy could guess what was in that bag—weed they liked to party with and probably the supply of Oxy and other things they enjoyed. She stayed out of that crap and as far as she knew, her father did too. Alexander had always been a concern to her, but she couldn't control him any more than her father could control her.

Her father waited till the pair disappeared inside the club before speaking to Dirty. His brow low, eyes narrowed. "You want to see my daughter."

"I do." Dirty didn't cower in the face of her father's glares.

"You aren't a Bighorn. Not even a new recruit."

"What does that matter, Dad? I can be with someone else. A rancher even."

Dirty met her gaze.

"Is that all he is? A harmless shit shoveler?" Her father grunted.

"I'm asking your permission to see more of Stormy, sir." Wes reached for her hand, and she entwined their fingers, clinging tight. She was on the verge of happiness or hell. But if her father sent Dirty away without his blessing, that didn't mean she wouldn't find a way to see him again.

And again.

He was in her system now.

Her father gave a hard nod. "I'll think on it. In the meantime…" He pointed at the road.

Dirty squeezed her fingers one more time and looked into her eyes. Then he released her and walked over to his bike, got on and rode away. She wanted to yell for him to take her too. The club didn't feel as free as it once had.

Chapter Four

Rivulets of sweat ran down Wes's spine, wetting his shirt. His muscles burned with each bale of hay he tossed onto the truck.

"How's it goin' down there, boys?" Uncle Matthias asked from his perch on the tractor that hauled the hay wagon.

Wes shot his cousins a look. The three of them had always hated haying season but more so as adults who realized their labor could be cut by the purchase of a machine that picked up the bales and shot them onto the wagon.

"Be better if you weren't such a cheapskate, Dad," Aiden grumbled.

"You missed one, Aiden." Matthias grinned as he pointed toward one Aiden hadn't picked up.

Wes hooked his gloved fingers under the twine of two more bales and hefted them. Walking behind the wagon this way and working this hard at least kept his mind off Stormy.

Or at least for a few minutes at a time.

He didn't want to think about what would happen if he returned to the club to hear Druid's response to him was no.

Wes didn't do no.

Especially when it came to Stormy.

After most of the hay was up and hauled back to the dry shed, Uncle Matthias dismissed them all to shower and rest. Aiden and Judd made a beeline for the house, but Wes hung back.

Matthias jumped off the tractor and faced Wes.

Sundance was the only man he'd suspected to be his father—except Uncle Matthias.

It all fit. They were about the same size, with the same dark hair and angled jaws. Their eyes the same steel gray. One time Wes had actually compared his hands to his uncles and thought they shared the same slightly bent forefinger.

But he couldn't speak the words.

"What's up, Wes? Didn't get enough of hayin'?"

"Well, I do wonder why you don't purchase better equipment."

He chuckled. "Maybe I like having my boys around me like old times."

My boys. Wes was a nephew. Wasn't he?

"The twins are so busy with their new wives that I miss the hell out of them. And you're spending more and more time at that club."

Wes looked down at the grass springing up around his boots. "Yeah." He'd spend a hell of a lot more time there if he could.

"Your aunt still hates it, I have to tell you," Matthias said.

Wes nodded. "She tells me every chance she gets."

"Seems there may be another reason you're spending so much time away lately. A woman?"

Snapping his head up, Wes met his uncle's stare. "Not just any woman."

Matthias's smile cut across his cheek in exactly the same way Wes's did. Nature or nurture? He had no fucking idea and wasn't ready to ask outright.

His uncle leaned against the tractor. "So this woman... I'm guessing she's worth your time."

"Oh yeah."

"I'm sensing there's a problem, though."

He always was good at rooting out troubles in him. As a kid, Wes rarely had to say what was on his mind before his uncle would bring it out in the open, much to Wes's relief.

"Bikers are close people. The Bighorns are the same. They don't mind me coming around, but they don't want me to spend time with this woman either."

"What's her name?"

"Stormy."

Matthias nodded. "Women named after seasons or acts of God can run you around good, believe me." He looked toward the house and the woman named Winter he'd spent a lifetime with.

"Her father's trying to stand in the way," Wes said.

"Daddies get protective of their daughters. Seen it with my own father when my sisters started dating."

"This is different. It's more old-fashioned than that. Like I don't belong to their society, so his daughter can't go outside the group."

"Does he have a man picked out for her already?"

Now that didn't sit well with Wes. He clenched his jaw—and his fists. "Not that I know of, but I wouldn't put it past him." He racked his brain for anybody he'd seen showing Stormy interest but could come up with no one.

"So you need to become one of them. Is that what you want?"

"I enjoy it, but I'd rather be at Eagle Crest."

He nodded. "So you have to show him that his daughter can have a life outside the club."

"No idea how to do that. Last time I took her on a ride, the guys surrounded my bike and forced us back."

"Don't like the sounds of that, but I trust you can handle yourself."

Wes nodded.

"Seems to me you have to get her away for a while and make her happy outside the club."

Wes met his uncle's—maybe his father's—stare. "Bring her here?"

Matthias clapped him on the shoulder and they started toward the house and cool glasses of iced tea. "I'm sure Judd'll thank you for bringing someone new around to get your aunt's mind off something besides Cecily's waistband. C'mon, son. Let's go inside and cool off."

Wes gave him a light punch on the arm. "Doesn't look as if you even broke a sweat."

His uncle leveled his gaze at him. "That's what I've got strong boys for."

* * * * *

"C'mon, Dirty." Druid grabbed his shoulder on his way to the door.

Alarms went off in his head but he got up and followed. Outside, two men flanked him, drawing weapons.

Dirty's pulse slowed. It wasn't the first time he'd been in a situation with armed men who disliked him. He'd come out alive then and he would now. Too bad he'd be taking out a few Bighorns in the process — that surely wouldn't get him closer to being on their good side and seeing more of Stormy.

"What is this? My sidearm's in my saddlebag."

"You won't need it. You can use mine." Druid slapped him on the back, but he didn't feel a hint of brotherhood in that touch. Was it pistols at dawn then? Or in this case pistols in midafternoon?

His mind went through the motions of disarming the men around him and incapacitating them. An elbow jab, knee to the balls, arm twisted upward to dislocate.

Nope — he wasn't dying today.

They crossed the yard as a group and rounded the garage where the bikes were stored. When he spotted Sundance and some of the others setting up targets, Wes almost laughed.

Druid shot him a glance, probably hoping to see him discomposed. Wes's years of hiding his emotions served him well now. He gave him a bland look in return.

"Let's see if you can shoot, Dirty." Druid held out a .44 Special on his hand. Too easy — all the Roshannons preferred a .44.

He accepted the weapon with a nod and aimed it away and to the ground as he checked the chamber. Locked and loaded. He waited till the Bighorns had the targets set to go and moved into position behind him.

"Let's see what you can do." Sundance sounded much less menacing than Druid. Then again, Wes and Sundance had found common ground from the start with his mother.

Wes took aim at the first target, a human figure with the rings on the chest and one on the forehead.

He squeezed off a shot and it hit where the eye would be.

Druid laughed. "He missed."

Wes gave him a crooked smile then directed another shot that punched through the target, creating a second eye. Then a nose. Finally, he shot one through the heart and one through the head.

Silence descended over the group and then Sundance said, "The boy can shoot."

Several chuckles sounded. Wes extended the weapon to Druid and nodded his thanks.

He started walking back to the club, but Druid stepped in front of him. "Now you need to know how I shoot."

"Why would I care about that?" He met the man's gaze.

"Don't let him scare you off, Dirty," Sundance said.

Wes hitched a thumb in his jeans pocket and watched as Druid reloaded and fired a perfect group through the heart of the human target. The ragged paper flapped in the mountain breeze.

When Druid turned and walked back inside without a word, Wes gave a low laugh. If he thought that was going to scare him off seeing Stormy, he didn't know anything about a man's determination.

Sundance grinned. "You passed the test, son."

"Is that so?"

"Yeah, you can shoot like a pro and didn't flinch when Druid challenged you. Other men haven't done so well."

"This is some sort of test to win his daughter?"

"No. Druid won't let you have her that easily if at all. But he might not growl as much when you look at her now."

Wes's lips tipped into a crooked smile. The guys continued with practice, but Sundance took him back into the club. When Wes saw what was going on in the main room, his instinct was to stop and look more closely. His years of hunting down criminals wasn't easily forgotten.

And the Bighorns were showing him how they really liked to party. The black duffle was set atop a table, the zipper open to reveal baggie after baggie of weed and prescription drugs.

Wes had suspected they were buying, dealing or both. But the fact that they were letting him see had to be another test.

He glanced up to see Druid watching him. Wes gave a chin nod to acknowledge him and moved to the table where he'd been sitting earlier staring at Stormy. Only she wasn't in the room—none of the women were. Did they ask them to leave when they got out the duffle?

Druid circled behind the bar and came out with two bottles of tequila. Fuck, Wes hated drinking games, but it seemed this might be another test.

He tried not to let out the sigh he was holding in. One thing he'd learned early in adulthood was that he was big enough to hold his liquor. If they were having a drink-you-under-the-table pissing contest, Wes would win hands down.

But besting Stormy's father at this wouldn't be a win for him any way he looked at it.

With a clank, Druid set a bottle before Wes. The guys zipped the bag and put it away again. Then they gathered around the table as Druid took a seat opposite Wes. He opened his own bottle and eyed Wes.

"I'm a beer man really."

Druid twisted his lips. "Beer's for pussies."

"Fine. How much are we drinking?" Wes picked up his bottle. He'd have a sour stomach and a hell of a headache tomorrow but there didn't seem to be any other course. If he walked away from Druid's challenge, the man would keep trying to best him.

"We drink till you pass out."

Wes nodded and raised the bottle to his lips. Before he took a sip, he lowered it and eyed Druid. "I don't think your daughter needs a man who can hold his liquor. I'd say having a man who can support and protect her is better."

Sundance's eagle eyes sharpened.

"Who said anything about my daughter?" Druid glared.

Wes glanced at the door, expecting to see Stormy there but she wasn't. He upended the bottle and swallowed the burning drink with smooth gulps.

When he set the bottle down again, it was one-third lighter. He waited while Druid did the same and they stared at each other. The liquor didn't take effect quickly, as Wes knew it wouldn't. He was still clear-eyed and clear-headed when Druid's speech began to slur.

"S'again," he said.

Resigned, Wes drank. Half an hour later, he was still upright and Druid listing to the left like a ship about to sink. Someone produced a knife and set it on the table between them.

Wes looked up, feeling hazier than usual but knowing if he had to get up and fight his way out of here, he could. "Are we carving our names in the table next?"

One guy laughed. "Wouldn't be fair — Druid's name has more letters."

"I see your point," Wes said dryly.

"Five finger fillet," the guy said.

Great. Now they wanted him to sacrifice a finger to prove himself. The knife game where you stabbed the table between your outstretched fingers wasn't going to end well.

Wes looked at Druid. "Is this really necessary?"

"Yesss."

Movement in the doorway drew Wes's attention and he barely realized what Stormy was doing until she plopped into his lap.

70

Her father didn't register what was happening at first, a testament to how the alcohol affected him. But Wes planted a hand on Stormy's side as she cuddled closer, her thigh riding close to his crotch, now bulging at the first feel of her weight on his lap.

She leaned in to whisper, "I can't let you lose a finger. When Dad drinks, there's no winning."

Wes reached up to brush the hair from her temple and then placed his mouth against her ear. "I need all my fingers to stroke your pussy."

A shiver ran through her and she steadied herself with a hand on his chest.

Finally, Druid's mind caught up to the situation. "That's my daughter. Get your hands off her!"

Stormy didn't move. "Dad, why don't you sleep it off?" She looked past him to the doorway where two women stood as if waiting for her cue. They came forward and each cozied up to Druid. In seconds, they were fawning over him and he forgot all about a drunken game of five finger fillet and his daughter being in the lap of a man he didn't want her with.

Stormy was resourceful, he'd give her that.

Sundance jerked his head toward the office off the main room. "Can I talk to you, Dirty?"

Reluctantly, he let go of Stormy, though he couldn't resist letting his hand linger on her hip as she got up.

Stormy threw him a concerned look as he followed their president. An office with a table large enough to seat eight members. The ruling body of the Bighorns.

The duffle sat on the table. Wes stared at it.

"I'm not going to ask you to make a run, Dirty."

He met Sundance's stare. "You know what happened to my mother." She'd OD'd on sleeping pills the Bighorns had probably provided to her.

He nodded. "And I was damn sorry for it." He lifted the bag to reveal two patches on the table. A new recruit and the arching insignia of the Bighorns.

Wes's chest constricted. This meant...

"They're yours, son. If you want them," Sundance said without hesitation.

Wes twitched to life. "I never expected it." He reached for the patches, sliding them across the shiny tabletop with two fingers.

"I know you probably thought Druid was just testing you for rights to his daughter."

Wes chuckled. "That's true."

"Over the past few weeks you've shown us that you'll be an asset to the Bighorns. That is if you want to become a member."

"I do," he said at once. Aunt Winter would hate it, but he had no intention of living any differently than he did now. Only having more time with Stormy.

"You've been helpful and proven yourself as loyal, though we got off in a bumpy way. We like having you around."

"I appreciate that."

Sundance extended a hand, which Wes shook. "I have to say I'm mighty fond of Stormy. Look at her like a favorite niece. I only want what's best for her."

Wes stiffened, on alert, prepared to be mowed down by Sundance as well.

But Sundance smiled. "If you're patched in, Druid won't have as many reasons to shoot you down."

A smile stretched Wes's mouth. "Now that I appreciate, Sundance. Very much."

"You're welcome. Now," he eyed Wes, "you know there's a run tonight and we don't leave our club or ladies without protection. Druid's down for the count, I'd say, and that only leaves you to look out for what belongs to us. I'm asking you to stay here and see that it happens."

"I'm your guy."

"I know you are. Just make sure come morning, there aren't any little baby Dirtys left behind, all right?"

At that, he laughed. "Got it."

As the president gestured for Wes to leave his office first, he couldn't help but feel a kinship toward the man he'd once suspected was his father. He was handing him so much—trust, an honored place

73

among them and his favorite "niece" all in one fucking awesome package.

Wes knew just how to celebrate such a sweet victory.

* * * * *

Stormy made a sound of surrender, and he didn't hesitate to pick her up and carry her into her room, still kissing her. She dug her fingers into his shoulders as he kicked the door shut, boot heel slamming off the wood with a cracking sound.

"Don't stop, Dirty."

His chest tightened with something more than lust. He couldn't afford to feel anything for a woman who didn't even know his real name, but he had no control over that sensation of warm, bubbling happiness.

He set her on her feet and they stared at each other.

"What did Sundance say to you?"

He shook his head. "Club business."

"I think you're growing on the Bighorns."

"It's the new recruit patch." As soon as Stormy had seen the patches, she'd whisked his cut away to the kitchen and later it was returned to him with the patches stitched on.

"I don't think that's the only reason." She slapped at him, but the abuse soon turned to murmured sighs as he cupped her breast, rubbing his thumb back and forth over the distended tip.

She hurled her arms around his neck, yanking him down to kiss him with a passion she'd never felt before. Tongues twirling, they tore at each other's clothes. She took off his cut with a reverence a Bighorn had for the sacred leather and patches he'd been given tonight in a short ceremony before the guys had left on their run.

He stripped her top overhead and her bra followed.

The instant her full breasts bounced free, he dipped his head to one, sucking the tip into his mouth. She moaned and slid her arms into the warm leather she'd just taken off him. He rolled his tongue around her nipple until it strained and then he grazed it with his teeth.

"God, yes. Your mouth feels so good, Dirty." She shimmied again, pulling on his leather cut.

"Fuck, you look gorgeous. The black leather against your pale skin makes me ache. God help me. I don't know if I can hold back," he rumbled.

"I'm not asking you to." She gripped the sides of the vest and parted it open for him to see her breasts.

He reached between his shoulder blades and pulled his shirt overhead. Her gaze danced over his chest. She stepped up to him and rested a hand in the center. "I love that you have chest hair. So manly."

He gripped her wrist and guided it down the planes of his abs to the bulge in his jeans. He pressed her hand harder to his throbbing erection and stared into her eyes. "Do you love this too, baby?"

"You know I do."

"Then get on your knees and suck it. Suck my cock while wearing my cut."

A spear of desire stabbed between her thighs as she sank to her knees before him. A dizzy wave of need overwhelmed her.

He grated out, "Unbuckle my belt and my jeans."

She worked over his fly and he fixed his gaze on her. She pulled his cock free and leaned in to skim the tip of his hard cock with her tongue. She flashed a look at his face to see his stare on her, eyes dark.

She swirled her tongue around and around, easing down the length until she had all of him in her mouth. Right to the root.

"Fucking hell," he growled.

Humming in response, she ran her lips up and down his hard length, pausing to suck the head with a soft pull of her lips, before repeating her explorations. He grunted and tensed, leaving only a primal beast who was putty in her hands.

She loved the power of that far too much.

As she continued to retrace the path from root to slit, he held his breath. She pushed his jeans and boxers down to his knees and sank her nails into his ass to pull him nearer. He watched her face as she brushed her lips against the trim hair at the base of his cock.

"Fuck."

She withdrew on his cock so only the tip was between her lips, clamped softly as she stroked her tongue over the tip. Pre-cum oozed from him, and she moaned.

Then she drew back, parting her lips so he could see the cum stretching between his body and her tongue.

"My God." He cupped her face and pulled her back down on him. "Look at me."

She flicked her gaze up to find the depths of his eyes burning with need.

"Bite down," he ordered, his voice sounding like grit.

Her eyes opened wider.

"Not too hard. Just use your teeth."

She'd never done such a thing. She wasn't that experienced in the first place, but what Dirty was asking wasn't typical either.

She wanted to give him everything he asked for and more.

She wrapped her fist around his cock at the base and opened wide to show him her teeth. When she grazed the head of his cock with them, he threw his head back on a groan. She ran her teeth down to the middle of his shaft and then back up. She didn't need to ask to know he liked what she was doing.

His legs shook with the effort to remain standing. "Fuck, don't stop what you're doing. It makes me want to give you my cut and helmet both." Each a symbol of what she meant to him.

As she moved back to the head, he urged her in a low voice to bite down again. She barely grazed him when he jerked away.

"Enough." He grabbed her by the hair, wound it around his fist and urged her to her feet.

Her nipples couldn't get any harder. She'd liked what he'd asked her to do. Liked his rough treatment of her too.

"I bet you're soaked for me, aren't you?"

She nodded, panting hard.

"Pull your pants down and let me see."

With another flash of her eyes, she stripped off her boots, socks, jeans and finally her panties. When she stood before him wearing only his leather and patches, her breaths came too fast.

"Pull your pussy open for me to see how wet you are."

"Oh my God, Dirty," she whispered on almost a plea.

He settled his gaze on her face. "Now."

Sliding her hands down to her thighs, she used her fingertips to pull her outer lips open. Revealing her slippery clit and inner folds.

"The road to heaven and hell," he muttered.

He picked her up and tossed her on his bed. She bounced only once before he pinned her thighs open and sank his tongue deep into her pussy.

A cry left her, followed by a long, throaty moan. He lapped in and out and then up and down her seam, just skimming her clit enough to drive her crazy.

"You liked sucking my cock, didn't you?" he asked between flips of his tongue.

"Ahhhh. Yes, Dirty."

"And did you like biting me?"

She trembled. "Yesss."

"You want to do it again, don't you?"

"Please."

"Just like you want me sucking your clit, but I won't." He ran his rough five o'clock shadow over her sensitive inner thigh.

"Please, Dirty. Right there. Oh God."

He pulled his tongue away from her clit again before she could enjoy it too much. She squirmed in his grip, trying to get where she wanted him most.

He sank his tongue into her wetness again and again. She was on fire for him.

When she bucked upward, he finally gave her what she asked for—he sucked her hard pearl into his mouth and drew on it with soft, insistent pulls.

It took her three point two seconds to scream his name. Another millisecond to explode in a half dozen pulsations.

Need swept her upward on the wave of her release and she had no conscious knowledge of him donning a condom, or moving over her and sinking his throbbing cock into her squeezing tight pussy until he was buried inside.

She gasped and looked into his eyes. "Move, Dirty," she rasped.

He braced himself over her and did five slow, grinding pushups. Sinking deeper with each pass. Her pussy clenched as that familiar sensation of heat about to rush upward.

He slid his hands beneath her ass and angled her just right. Another scream ripped from her as she squeezed him with her inner muscles. His movements grew disjointed and she knew he was losing it.

The first jet that left him tore a growl from his throat. The next three made her see stars again and by the sixth spurt, he collapsed atop her. His lips found hers and they shared a slow, lingering kiss.

Fuck, she was in so much trouble.

It didn't stop her from kissing him back with all the pent-up passion she was feeling. Slow passes of their tongues soon turned into hungrier, eager kisses and she straddled him to give herself two more orgasms.

When he rolled her over and took her again, something inside her heart broke open.

On the heels of that thought was, *Hell, now what?*

Chapter Five

Wes's adrenaline didn't normally hit a high like this during a foot chase, but it was pumping like a Yellowstone geyser. His leg muscles burned, and his lungs were on fire with a pent-up roar.

When he lengthened his strides, he was unmatchable, but the asshole in his sights had gone from wanted list to Wes's personal vendetta list and he had a head start.

Didn't mean anything. In two minutes max, Wes would have him on the ground even without a taser.

Van Atkins was determined not to be caught, but Wes was ending this today. *Enjoy your last bit of freedom, dickhead. Because today is the last you'll breathe the fresh mountain air for a long time.*

He hurdled a garden bed, his boot coming down in the soft earth of the corner, and pushed off faster. He might be a big motherfucker, but he could run. Fast. Years of track had taught him how to use his size as a way to propel himself. He pumped his arms and closed the gap.

Van ducked inside a carport and went out the other side, and Wes was right behind. This was the trouble with being in a residential neighborhood — more obstacles. But Wes wasn't losing this guy again.

Skidding on gravel on the other side of the carport, he feared he'd lose precious seconds, but it actually gave him another few inches of lead.

And the guy ahead of him was no match for Wes's long arm.

He snagged his sleeve and yanked, ripping the man off his feet. He hit the ground with a grunt but had enough wits to throw a punch.

It glanced off Wes's ear, making it ring and him madder.

Damn, but he'd like to lay into the guy. But brute force wasn't even a possibility because Wes didn't have much handle on his control after all Atkins had dealt him. He had to keep it together.

He crushed Van's thigh under his knee, pinning one limb while he made a grab for his hands. He preferred long zip-ties to handcuffs and he could snug them up as much as he needed.

In this case, he went a bit tighter than usual just for the added aggravation of hunting Van the entire past year.

"Owww, you bastard," Van howled.

"Shut up. You're lucky this is all I'm doing to you. I owe you for that punch to my ear."

Van kicked, and Wes flattened him beneath his body. He had fifty pounds on him easy.

"Now, we are going to stand up and you're going to walk nice and slow to my truck. Got it?"

He jerked his elbows to try to free his wrists but only managed to harm himself in the process as the plastic tie dug into his flesh. "Fuck you!"

"No thanks. You ain't my type." He pushed to his feet and dragged Van up with him. The guy wobbled to stay upright, and Wes straightened him out.

"Now walk." When the man didn't move, Wes kicked at the heel of Van's boot. "Go!"

Reluctantly, he moved forward—for two steps. Then he tried to do a drop and roll to break free.

"Dammit, you're not too bright, are you?" Wes dug a knee into his back and got out his rope.

Van twisted his neck and eyed him. "What the fuck are you doin' with that?"

"In case you don't know my reputation, I can string up an animal or man faster than you can think to take a step. Wanna play?"

"No."

"Too bad." He created a slipknot and dropped it over Van's head so it settled around his chest. When he gave a hard yank, the rope tightened and Van bellowed. Struggled. He fell over and Wes hauled him back up.

"Try that again and I'll hogtie and drag you to the truck."

"I'll hit you with charges of police brutality."

"I'm not police and nobody would care how I got you before the judge, since you've been evading arrest for a year now. Get your ass movin'." He kicked his boot again.

Reluctantly, Van stumbled forward. Wes wrapped the end of the rope around his fist, prepared to restrain him if he attempted to run again. But Van just spewed threats instead.

"Fucking kill you in your sleep, Roshannon."

"Nice, Atkins. When you plan on doin' that? After you get out five years from now? You had a petty charge of shoplifting but now you're looking at hard time for all the other crimes you've been committing. I heard you've stolen two vehicles at least on top of the shoplifted DVDs. I hope to hell that 'Ghostbusters Anniversary Edition' was worth it."

Wes had chuckled at the list of stolen DVDs back when he'd seen it and he couldn't help but smile at his jab.

"Asshole."

"Take that as a compliment."

"I'll hunt you down when I get out."

"Like to see you try."

"I'll find your family. Your wife and kids."

"Don't have those." Though an image of Stormy as he'd last seen her flitted through his head. The way her eyes glowed at him as he sucked her hard nipples was a distraction he didn't need at the moment.

"Your ma and pa then. I'll kill them in their beds."

Wes gave a harsh laugh. "Don't have those either. Now shut your trap, Atkins. You're boring me."

The exchange got to him, and he didn't want to admit it. He'd been ignoring the whole paternity question for far too long now. Soon he'd have to make the choice — forget about it forever or confront the last person who could be responsible for baby Wes.

He tightened his jaw and focused on getting this son of a bitch to the truck. He secured him with straps in the back seat to make sure he couldn't break free. Then he tried to shut out Van's bullshit threats and curses against Wes's very soul as he drove to the sheriff's office.

When he dumped the asshole off, the sheriff clapped him on the back and offered to buy him a steak.

"I'll accept that for another time, sheriff. Thank you. I need to get back to the office. Damon has an assignment for me."

The drive took less than a minute, and Wes put all the windows down to air out the stink of Van Atkins from his truck. After he parked, he didn't bother putting the windows up either. It would take a gale wind and a can of air freshener to get the scent of onions and BO out.

As he approached the door of the building, his boss Damon was standing there with a shit-eating grin on his face. "Heard you got Atkins."

"Yeah, the dickhead is way more trouble than he's worth."

Damon held out his fist for Wes to bump with his knuckles. "Nice job."

He'd brought in hundreds of fugitives in his years as a bounty hunter, yet his boss had never greeted him at the door.

"What's going on?" He eyed Damon.

"Got something big."

"I figured if you called me in."

"Come inside. I'm not discussing it out here."

The place smelled like copier ink and scorched coffee, which Damon offered him as they passed the pot.

"No thanks," he muttered.

Damon led him into his small office. The whole operation was small but was one of the most well-known in the West. His boss took up his chair behind his desk and stared at Wes, his cowboy hat settled in that cocky way Damon had of wearing it.

"Just say what's on your mind," he said without beating around the bush.

Damon shifted a few papers around and came up with a sheet bearing an unfamiliar photograph.

He reached for the sheet and stared at the photo of a guy he might have seen before but couldn't place where. "What's the story?" he asked his boss.

Damon kicked back as if getting comfy for a long tale. "Trouble on the rez."

"Theft?"

"Drug-related crimes. Someone is supplying some members of the tribe with prescription drugs."

Oh fuck. Prescription drugs.

It could be anyone.

Not the Bighorns.

"Our suspect's already on the lam. Was arrested back in November for drug possession with the intent to sell. Out on bail, his father's doing. Now he's on the radar of the rez cops. They want him bagged and tagged so they can control the drug problem they already battle on the rez."

"We have a name?"

Damon nodded. "Alexander Bonner."

Wes's fingers tingled with relief. He'd never heard the name. "Any idea where to find him?"

"Now that's your job, ain't it, Wes?" Damon grinned. "But yeah, there's a lead. He's in this biker club called the Bighorns."

Wes felt his blood slowly drain from his heart to pool in his stomach, leaving him queasy. His knee-jerk reaction that this was the doing of a Bighorn was spot-on. Fucking hell, he hated being right all the time.

"How do you know he's in a club?"

"He's seen wearing their patch on his leather vest."

"Cut," he automatically corrected.

His boss raised a brow. Nobody besides his family knew Wes had been spending time with the Bighorns.

"Okay, you seem to know a little about this world. You'll know right where to look. Easy money in your pocket."

"Yeah, easy money." The hard way. He'd be betraying the people he'd come to think of as friends and hauling away one of their own wouldn't earn him any points with Stormy.

Damon was looking at him too closely. Wes stood and turned for the door.

"You know them."

Without looking back, he gave a nod to Damon's question. "I know where I can find them."

Wes went outside and got in his truck. He drove without conscious thought to direction. He just needed to get out of here, see the mountains.

Fucking hell. His bounty was a Bighorn? He didn't know anybody named Alexander Bonner, but then again he only knew nicknames and almost no last names were used among the crew. For all he knew, his bounty was Stormy's father.

He had some decisions to make.

For the first time ever, he could ignore a bounty set before him and let someone else find Bonner.

Or he could dig a little deeper and try to get the guy out quietly, without anybody discovering he was responsible. Bonner would just suddenly disappear and they'd hear through the grapevine he'd been captured.

He reached back through the memories of all those parties and all the Bighorns he'd come in contact with. The Green Hills chapter had ridden with them and co-hosted several events during the time Wes had been involved in the club. He could pluck nearly every name from his memory on cue—and those he couldn't remember would be pulled to the surface as soon as he saw a face.

There was no way he'd ever been introduced to Alexander Bonner.

Hell. He was in a touchy predicament. He felt a hard-core loyalty to the club, wore their fucking patches now. They'd accepted him, and now he was going to betray that trust by searching within their own group for the fugitive he hunted.

* * * * *

Perfume. Not just any perfume but *cheap* perfume, the kind that burned your nose hairs and made you think of seedy bars and strip clubs.

Wes's nose was filled with the odor, so thick he could almost taste it.

It definitely wasn't Stormy's scent.

He'd gone to bed alone, unable to get Druid off his tail long enough to even give Stormy a goodnight kiss. So who was this person plastered against his side, naked?

He opened his eyes to see the bleach-blonde passed out next to him. The bikers called these women sweet butts, but he didn't see much sweet about 'em — women who slept with anybody wearing leather. It was sad, really, but Wes had seen worse.

How the fuck had she landed in his bed? He sure as hell hadn't invited her.

All at once he realized she'd been sent to him. By Druid.

He bolted upright.

The sweet butt moaned and grabbed her stomach.

Wes shoved her. "Don't puke in my bed! Go to the bathroom!"

She stumbled and lurched across the room, half-naked and too skinny. She made it to the door and into the hallway before he heard her retch.

The disgusting scent of vomit hit him, and he groaned. "What I wouldn't give for a breath of clean ranch air," he muttered, thinking of Eagle Crest. He got up and closed the door.

He'd fallen into bed wearing jeans and boots, a habit he'd formed from his job. He never knew when he'd have to hit the ground running — literally. He located a black T-shirt and his cut slung over the back of a chair. The leather sported a brand-new full member patch. He was now a Bighorn.

He caught a glimpse of himself in the mirror beside the door. Black hair, black stubble on his jaw, black clothing right down to his steel-toed shit-kickers. The only thing that wasn't black were his eyes, and they were damn close.

He opened the door to find the sweet butt on her hands and knees with a bucket and cloths, cleaning up her own sick mess. She looked up at him, eyes bloodshot and blonde hair falling into one eye.

"Sorry, Dirty. I didn't mean to almost puke in your bed." Her voice was raspy around his nickname, her words still slurred. She was still drunk and probably would be till noon.

He wanted to ask who the hell had sent her there in the first place, but she didn't need to be involved in Druid's game anymore.

"Next time try not to drink so much," he said as he walked out of his room and shut the door.

He made it outside and to fresh air. He closed the door of the club and leaned against the wall, dragging in deep breaths of the mountain air.

The club sat high up where a man could think and see clear to the next state, and the views reminded him of Eagle Crest. Damn, he missed home.

"Dirty." The grating voice made him turn.

"Sundance," Wes said with a nod of acknowledgement.

The guy's face was craggy from a hard night of partying, but his blue eyes never missed a thing.

"Smoke?" Sundance removed a pack of cigarettes from the pocket of his cut and shook a few loose.

Wes shook his head. "Need a drink before I smoke. Cotton-mouth," he lied. Thing was, he hated lying to Sundance. The man was one of the good old boys.

Sundance chuckled, the sound like tearing paper from decades of smoking. "Hard drinking'll do that to ya. The keg against the far wall inside isn't empty yet."

"Nah, not for breakfast." Wes shot him a smile. "What are you doin' out here so early?"

"Just seein' my lady off. She's headed home for another week. Got the grandbabies coming and she'll be babysitting while our oldest daughter's on a business trip." Sundance had a strangely normal family—who he lived apart from, up here in the mountains, away from those he claimed to love the most. And that would be his wife of thirty years.

Wes nodded and turned to look over the snowy tips of the mountains spread out before them. "Sounds like a real fun time."

"Oh yeah, Darlene loves those grandbabies somethin' fierce."

Wes didn't ask if Sundance did too. He did in his own way, Wes supposed.

But the talk of family made him miss his own.

Sundance pushed out a heavy sigh. "A man can't get closer to his Maker than in these mountains, can he, Dirty?"

"Pure peace," Wes agreed, only half meaning it. He loved the mountains and enjoyed the club and fellow brothers, at least when he wasn't supposed to locate one of them and haul him in to face criminal charges.

He wanted to return to Eagle Crest—take Stormy with him. But getting her away would have the Bighorns tailing him and that meant they'd learn he was a Roshannon. Then know what he did for a living. Odd they'd accepted him as one of their own without asking many questions. It seemed knowing he could shoot and hold his tequila was enough. The biker culture had its own code, and if you were loyal, they didn't care what you did in your spare time.

Then again, he hardly knew what any of the Bighorns did for a living either. They came and went from the club, and he assumed many had jobs, but they didn't discuss it and nobody asked.

First and foremost, he was a Roshannon. And a bounty hunter.

Before he left for Eagle Crest, he needed to figure out who Alexander Bonner was.

Aunt Winter would be upset—he hadn't been home in too long. He'd been busy. Wanted to spend time with Stormy.

Or maybe he was hiding from his real reason for not going home.

"I'd love to get on two wheels," Wes said. Wyoming weather was unpredictable as hell, and the clouds banking in the West heralded bad weather.

Sundance clapped him on the shoulder. "Rain's comin'. I feel it in my leg." He tapped his fingers against the thigh of his leg that had more plates and screws than most foreign cars could boast. "You're just like your mother. Never could sit still for long."

Wes's throat clogged off, just as it always did at mention of his momma. But lately more so when he thought of his uncle—and what the man could really be to him.

"Yeah, I can't sit around here all day. I've gotta be on the open highways." Wes held out a hand to Sundance, and they clasped fists in the way of the club brothers.

"Give 'em hell, Dirty. Take as many prisoners as you fucking can."

Sundance didn't know how true his words rang.

* * * * *

Stormy set down the handfuls of bags she'd driven into town for, aggravated that her father had sent her on such a stupid errand. The list he'd given her was ridiculous, with a mix of food items and things she could only get at a hardware store, seemingly unrelated.

It wasn't the first time she'd been sent on a club errand, yet she couldn't help but feel they were keeping her away for a reason.

"Where's Dirty?" she asked as soon as DeeDee looked up from the tabloid she was reading.

"Look who it is!" DeeDee smiled too brightly. Or was that Stormy's imagination?

DeeDee pushed back to stare at her. "Oh my God, girl, you're more beautiful than ever. That crisp air agrees with you. Come sit down and I'll get you some hot coffee."

Ignoring the bags she'd dumped on the kitchen floor, she crossed the room to the table.

"Now sit right down here and we'll have a good talk over coffee. Never get enough girl time, do we?"

Stormy shrugged. DeeDee was always exuberant but this might be overkill. She looked at her friend closer.

DeeDee set a steaming mug on the scarred wooden table before her.

"Thanks for the coffee. What's been going on around here today?"

"Same old. Lynn fusses about making the beer runs and the bitch is about to get kicked out. You know not pulling your weight's a crime around here."

Stormy watched the door of the kitchen, eager to go find Dirty. They hadn't been alone in too long, and she'd been burning for his touch all night long, hoping he'd come to her door. But the party had raged on till morning and she hadn't gotten a chance to slip into his room either.

DeeDee was quiet. Strangely quiet.

"Shit. What is it?" Stormy asked.

DeeDee didn't respond at first. Silence hung in the air like a heavy weight.

Her friend rested a hand on her forearm and Stormy looked up, dread hitting her chest. "Some things have been going on, Stormy."

Oh fuck. "What is it? Did my dad start shooting holes in the walls again?" Her voice wobbled.

DeeDee's eyes were ringed with concern.

She stared at her friend.

"Dirty had a woman in his—"

Before DeeDee could get the words out, Stormy pushed away from the table, leaping to her feet. Her cup rocked, sloshing coffee all over the surface. Pain stabbed her. She and Dirty had never committed to each other, but there was an unspoken rule that neither was sleeping around.

"Don't get so upset, Stormy. This shit happens with men. They have needs…"

"Jesus, you don't really believe that crap, do you, Dee? That men can't stay faithful and keep their peckers in their pants for a few days?"

"Well—"

Fury rose up. "Who was it?" Figured as soon as she had two minutes alone to think that she wanted a life outside the club—and Dirty—that he'd go fuck someone else.

Her friend eyed her like she was a ticking bomb.

"Tell me or I'll find someone who can."

"No, no. You want to hear this from me."

Stormy gaped at her. That could only mean the worst. "It was Spazz."

"No, not Spazz."

Stormy narrowed her eyes at her friend and stalked around the table to stand over her. "DeeDee, who told you when that whore from the other chapter was after Sam? I always got your back. Now you'd better have mine."

"Damn, you know how to hurt a woman. You know you're my best friend, Stormy."

She pushed out a sigh and closed her eyes for a second before opening them again, temper more in hand. At least until she thought of some slut's hands on Dirty. "The name," she demanded.

"Kylie."

Her jaw might have hit the floor. But the pain was in her chest. "That whore? Dirty put his hands on her?"

I will not lose my shit. There are no promises between us.

Just a whole lot of chemistry and some stupid feelings I need to shut down.

Her chest felt like it was being flayed open by betrayal.

She was so dumb to believe what they had was something more.

Except when they were alone, his kisses blazing over her lips, she belonged to him in the way only a woman could belong to a man.

"He fucked that skinny bitch?" Her words came out breathless, her heart racing too fast to give her a chance to draw air.

DeeDee stood and caught her arm, surprisingly strong for her size. "She came out of his room, that's all we know. I guess we don't know that he fucked her."

"And where exactly is *he*?"

"He rode out this morning."

"On one of his vanishing acts again?"

DeeDee nodded.

It bothered her that she didn't know where he went, and he didn't tell her. But it was clear she was far more invested in this non-relationship than he was. She figured he went back to his ranch to help the uncle he'd mentioned, but now her mind whirled around the possibility that he had a girlfriend, fiancée or wife somewhere.

She could hardly breathe. "And where can I find Kylie?"

Tightening her grip, DeeDee shook her head. "You can't kill her. It's her job to be here for the guys."

Stormy loved this club. But if she stayed with the Bighorns until she was a hundred, she'd never understand this twisted thinking that a man could fuck anyone in his path simply because he had a big engine between his legs.

Stormy strode out of the kitchen. Behind her, she heard DeeDee's chair tip in her haste to rush after her. In the main room, a group of guys had just come in, cold still clinging to them and a draft racing through the space.

"Welcome back, Stormy. Looks like you're in a twister state of mind," her dad joked.

"Where'd Dirty go?" she demanded.

Her father looked her over, his eyes full of the same concern she'd seen on DeeDee's face. "Don't know. Just left as always. This about Kylie?"

Stormy's chest felt like someone had ratcheted a cable around it. She didn't want to think about why that was—she just wanted to know the truth. "Does everyone know about him and Kylie?"

Four other guys turned their gazes on her. All at once, she realized she couldn't do this. This jealous woman was not her.

She ran her fingers through her hair. DeeDee took her by the shoulders and led her back into the kitchen. For five minutes, she listened to her friend talk nonsense about how they might not have fucked, but Stormy was finished caring. If he wanted to bone all these skinny sluts, then let him. She didn't need him.

Even if he gave her orgasms that made her view constellations up close and personal.

Not to mention making her feel excited about finding a new path in her life.

She slumped in her chair and DeeDee stopped talking. Her friend caught her gaze. "You okay, sweetie?"

Sure. She just had to figure out how to guard her heart against one muscled hulk of a man with dark gray eyes that could slay with a single glance.

"I'm fine." She chewed her lip. "What needs done around here?" She needed to take her mind off Dirty.

"Big party midweek. Green River chapter's coming for a spring ride."

"Does that mean Alexander's coming?"

DeeDee shrugged. "Could be. We'll be ready to give him a big homecoming if he is."

A few months ago she'd be thrilled to see her brother again, but now with all that was going on, she was too distracted to care as much.

"Tell me what needs to be done."

"Couple of us are going into town to get supplies."

Stormy cast a look at the bags she'd just brought in and one woman was now emptying. "What the hell did I just buy then?"

DeeDee looked away and then back. "You know we need a lot of food and liquor to host the Green Hills crew."

"I guess." She was past caring. "I'll help in a few. I just need a minute alone." Stormy had been about to burst into noisy tears since hearing Dirty had Kylie in his bed. But she was not going to waste a drop on that asshole.

She walked toward her room, not even gracing Dirty's door with a glance.

The fucker. Worse than her out-of-control feelings was the fact she never thought Dirty to be that man. For some reason, he'd seemed different. Because of that, she'd believed she could have a different life with him.

Not that she didn't love the Bighorns, her father and all the people who'd become family to her. But she was sick of the same thing day in and day out. Chores, parties. The world was bigger and she wanted a piece of it.

Dirty could have shown it to her. They could have explored it together.

She didn't know this side of him. Why now, after all this time? What had changed?

Hell with it. She didn't need him. Didn't need —

102

Warm arms encircled her from behind. She froze dead, her hand mid-reach for the doorknob to her room.

"Fuck, you look good." Dirty's chest rumbled against her back. Her ass fit oh, so perfectly against his groin. And his bulging erection said he felt it too.

She couldn't draw breath for fear of screaming out all the hurt. But worse, she couldn't risk smelling him.

Leather, spice and man. That combination was lethal to her senses.

She breathed shallowly through her mouth. He wrapped her closer to his body and skated his lips across the side of her neck. She panted harder.

"I thought you left," she choked.

Knee him in the balls or wrap her arms around his neck? The decision was a no-brainer after what he'd done.

He landed his kiss next to her ear, sending shudders of pleasure through her body. Her nipples hardened. As if knowing this, he cupped her breasts. Stroked his thumbs back and forth over the points distending her top.

Her knees weakened, and she ached to turn into his arms and look up into those gray eyes.

Just to be slaughtered all over again?

He'd hurt her and was hurting her now by pretending she meant something more than a wet pussy around his cock.

She jerked her arm back, ramming her elbow into his rock-hard midsection. A puff of air left him, and her arm tingled from the blow. She threw herself into her room and slammed the door in his face.

She didn't have time to lock it before he blasted in. The wood sounding as if it splintered on the hinges.

"What the hell's going on?" He slammed the door and locked it. Then legs braced wide, he stared at her.

Backing up a step, she threw out, "I thought you were gone."

"I'm back." He took a step closer.

She inched away. The room was small and soon she'd bump into the bed or dresser. In the space, Dirty looked like one toss of his hair out of his eyes would cave in a wall. His power, his steel-eyed look...

Oh God. Don't give in, Stormy.

She swallowed hard and braced herself for battle.

The backs of her thighs hit the soft mattress. Crap, the only way out was up through the small window or the door behind Dirty. Neither seemed like a good option.

"Baby, why are you looking at me that way?"

"Why don't you ask Kylie?" She hated the way her lower lip threatened to tremble on the words. She'd never been in love before, and she was not going to even consider the L word with a dickhead like Dirty.

His rugged features smoothed and he stared at her with understanding clear on his face. "Stormy. Baby, calm down. Nothing happened."

Sure. "Except you took a sweet butt into your bed!" Her voice escalated louder with each word. She was losing her shit. And why? Over a man. She was a Bighorn, dammit, not shaken apart by something so stupid and fragile as love.

Nope, not love. No L word within the same hemisphere as this biker.

He reached for her. Big hands closed over her upper arms and he drew her onto tiptoe, his mouth hovering inches from hers. Dammit, she'd taken a deep breath and now her head was swimming with his scent. All that spice and leather. God, how was she going to get to the window and open it before he caught her and she drowned in his scents again?

Head whirling, she looked away.

He pinched the point of her chin lightly and brought her gaze back. He had to have the fullest lips in the universe, didn't he? She closed her eyes.

"Stormy, look at me."

She'd spent too many nights in his bed taking his commands to not obey.

She opened her eyes, and the sight of his stare sucker-punched her.

He palmed her cheek, his hand extending from temple to jaw. She resisted the urge to lean into his touch.

"Baby, I didn't sleep with Kylie. Didn't even touch her."

She narrowed her eyes. "I'm supposed to believe that? I—"

His mouth crashed over hers in a bruising, consuming kiss. She parted her lips on a gasp and he thrust his tongue into her mouth. Hot, claiming. She pushed closer to him, her hands betraying her by grabbing his face to pull him down for more.

A moan echoed through the room, part hers, part his as they tumbled down on her bed. The springs protested his bulk, but she pawed at his shirt while he unbuttoned her jeans with a flick of his fingers.

She barely had time to think as he eased down her zipper and he pushed through denim and cotton to find her needy folds, wet and ready since the moment she set eyes on him.

Damn him to hell.

She bit into his lower lip and he growled. Grabbing her by the wrists and pinning her to the bed, he braced himself over her and glared. "I didn't fuck Kylie."

"How'd she end up in your bed then?"

"I don't have a fucking clue. I woke up and she was there, but I wasn't drunk, baby. I know I didn't lay a hand on her."

Her mind worked over this. Was it possible the woman had just taken it upon herself to slip into Dirty's bed? Or—

"You really didn't invite her in or fuck her?"

He shook his head. "She woke up ready to puke and I kicked her out into the hall before she could. That's it. Now are you done giving me the evil eye, Stormy, because I'm burning up."

"My dad." Her whisper came out on a puff of furious air.

Braced on his elbows, he leaned back to stare down into her eyes. "You think he set this up to make you mad at me?"

"I know he did. Revenge for siccing those two women on him and getting him away from the tequila."

"Damn, he's a twisted fucker."

"He isn't out to hurt me, Dirty. He just doesn't want me with you."

"And that doesn't hurt you? Never mind," he said before she could respond.

She gazed into his eyes. Her breaths came faster. She strained against his hands, wanting to touch him. "Swear it to me, Dirty. Swear you didn't have anything to do with Kylie."

His eyelids fluttered. "I swear, baby. On my mother's grave."

She made a sound of surrender, and he rocked his hips against hers.

Chapter Six

Having Stormy beneath him again, even biting and scratching, was the closest thing to heaven that Wes could imagine. Better than Eagle Crest on a warm summer's day, better than his aunt's biscuits after hard work.

Her warm, silky skin stole his control and Jesus Christ, was she wet for him. He moaned against her lips, and she answered by rocking upward.

He couldn't strip her fast enough. They ripped at each other's clothes. Her bra strap broke, sending them both giggling like teenagers. Then he had her spread before him.

"I'm going to fucking feast on this beautiful body," he grated out.

Her hips swelled outward, perfect for filling his big hands. Her waist narrowed and then flared up to full breasts he couldn't get enough of.

Bending over her, he took her nipple in his mouth. She sucked in a gasp and locked a hand over his nape to pull him down harder.

He flicked his tongue over the tip of her breast. A spasm hitting his groin as her nipple hardened for him.

"So fucking responsive. Tell me how it feels." He grazed her nipple with his teeth, raising a shudder from her.

She twisted her fingers in his hair as he sucked at her nipple with strong pulls of his lips. "Feels so fucking good. Don't stop."

"Like this?" He locked his gaze on hers while drawing on her taut bud. When he finished with a tongue swirl that made her eyes roll up in her head, he moved to the other with a satisfied smirk.

His balls throbbed and he couldn't wait to bury himself deep in her wet heat. He wasn't letting her leave this bed before he'd had his fill.

Starting with her nipples and ending with his face between her round thighs.

She watched him torment her other nipple, speaking in incoherent coos and moaned words. He moved to kissing the flat of her belly, and she arched off the bed. He grinned against her golden skin, working his way down to the treasure nestled between her thighs.

When his tongue met her sweetness, his cock hardened to full mast. Throbbing against the mattress, he fought down his own urges as he set to work.

Nibbling the creases of her inner thighs until she wriggled. Brushing kisses over her outer pussy lips until she writhed. All the time avoiding the place she most wanted him.

As impatient as ever, she grabbed him by the hair and pushed him toward her clit.

"Lick my pussy, Dirty. You're not doing your job."

"Oh, I think I'm doing a fucking great job." He resisted teasing that bundle of nerves, watching desire play over her features.

"Dirty." His name came out as a warning and a moan.

He let his breath wash over her neediest spot. "You want me to taste you here?" He lowered his head until he barely grazed her clit.

"Oh God!" She bucked upward, pressing her pussy into his mouth.

He took control, gripping her ass and feasting on her with tongue, lips and even applying pressure against her opening with his jaw.

"God, I love when you face-fuck me."

"Less talk," she mewled, inner thigh muscles twitching around his ears.

He slipped one finger into her soaking pussy. She cried out as he sank it deep, curling his fingertip up toward her inner wall and stroking her G-spot.

She vibrated with every stroke, and he felt her coming apart long before the rhythmic clench and release of her pussy began.

"Dirty... please. Faster! Yes!"

He pounded her and flattened his tongue over her straining nubbin, reveling in her flavors as she stiffened and started to pulsate.

Three hard contractions… four. She quivered under his mouth, but he didn't let up his assault until he'd ripped three more contractions from her.

He lifted his head and pinned her with a wolfish grin.

"Get that condom on, Dirty. I can't wait for you long."

He pushed to his knees and gripped his cock at the base. Fisted it once, nice and slow, as she watched.

When she licked her thumb and ran the pad over his slit, he issued a guttural groan. Who the fuck was he kidding? He couldn't resist her any more than she could him.

He grabbed that condom and rolled it into place in seconds. As he spread her legs wide and angled her body up to accept him, he looked into her eyes.

"Tell me you want me," he rasped.

Her eyes, big, chocolate brown and burning with life, met his. "You know I do. Why do you think I got so mad about Kylie?"

"I haven't touched anyone but you." He dropped his forehead to hers. "I never pretend when I'm alone with you." He took his cock in hand and rubbed the swollen head over her slick folds. His balls clenched tight to his body, aching with the need to feel her wrapped around his every inch.

Using her heel on his ass, she jerked him into her at the same moment she bucked up to meet him.

He sank balls-deep. Eyes closing on a prayer for control he couldn't seem to find when he was with her.

She cupped his face and kissed his brow, his nose, his cheeks and finally his mouth. "Take me."

There was something in those words that touched his heart, a warm lick against a cold, lonely chunk of granite.

He ground his hips, cock head rubbing her deepest point.

"Oh my God... please do that again."

He did, watching her face contort with bliss.

Then he grabbed her hair in one fist and tilted her head back to suck the pulse hammering in her neck while pounding into her body. She clung to him, her pussy grabbing at his every stroke, and he was losing his goddamn mind.

In seconds, he was driving faster, harder, uncaring who heard his grunts or her screams as that familiar warm heat coiled at the base of his spine, telling him he was about to blow.

Reaching between their bodies, he pressed his thumb over her clit, helping her along.

In two more strokes, she was shaking in his hold with her release, and he spurted into her tight heat. Mind-numbing pleasure stole over him for God knew how long, and he came up for air to find her staring at him.

She brushed his heavy hair off his brow in that tender way she always did after coupling, but this time he saw something more in her gaze.

She was going to hate him, like all the other Bighorns, when he found the man he hunted and revealed who he truly was.

* * * * *

The big garage was packed with guys working on their bikes, tuning them up to ride. Looking around at the brothers, he felt part of it all.

His bike was parked toward the back, and the steel and chrome called to him. He'd never completely go back to pickups and horses now — he loved the speed and freedom of riding motorcycle.

And he loved the Bighorns. Which was why it was going to be so hard to capture Bonner.

The guys issued a rowdy guffaw of laughter, and he grinned at their antics. Ribbing the new club members was part of the feeling of family — something he missed with his cousins. Yeah, he needed to head to Eagle Crest and soon.

After what he planned to do to the Bighorns, he'd be banned anyway. It grated on him, but when he thought of Stormy, it sliced him deep. He had no idea how to keep her and do this job.

113

Sundance waved him over, and Wes angled through the bikes, scattered toolboxes and jugs of oil to reach the prez's side.

"Mother Nature's a fickle bitch in these mountains. Think the weather'll hold out for the ride?" Wes leaned against the nearby wall and folded his arms.

Sundance gave a nod. "Better hold out or we'll need more booze and women to occupy them all."

Sundance stared at him.

"Somethin's on your mind. Speak it," Wes drawled out.

"You left mighty quickly yesterday and returned just as quick."

Wes lifted a shoulder and let it fall. "Thought I needed to escape the confines of the club, but I realized I wasn't wrong."

Sundance eyed him. "Can't help but wonder what a man like you's searchin' for."

Wes kept up his lazy pose, but his heart picked up the pace. Last thing he needed was a group of bikers pissed off that he'd snowed them over more than the Wyoming winter.

Sundance continued to work, picking up various tools and tweaking his bike engine as he talked. "You came here searching for your mother's story."

"That's true. And I see why she felt this club was home."

"The brothers of this club all have stories too. Some worse than others, but we've all seen battle of some sort. I just wonder what you've seen." Sundance's blue eyes settled on Wes.

He pushed off the wall and crouched next to the bike where Sundance was working. "Seen some things, but like you said, not more than any other Bighorn." What was he fishing for?

Sundance nodded again. "You've got other questions, though, which is why you leave. You're searching for something."

Yeah, fugitives.

He controlled his expression and counted his breaths to keep from giving himself away. These bikers may be his friends now, but as soon as they discovered he was using them, he wouldn't last long.

And Stormy would hate him.

Wes gave a low chuckle. "Searching for the meaning of life, you mean? Shit like that?"

Sundance's mouth twisted in his idea of a smile. "Was thinking more about searching for your pa."

Wes's spine snapped straighter. "My father?"

"Yeah, you've never been told who he is, right?"

Now his mouth was dry and his heart thundering. He tried for some semblance of nonchalance. "That's right. You know him?"

Sundance dropped his wrench into the toolbox. "Nah. He wasn't anybody I knew. Your momma was knocked up when she came to us. On the run, like someone was chasing her, but I always suspected it was her personal demons and not a true threat."

"So my father was outside the club."

"Yep." He nodded again. Always nodding, like his neck was on a spring. "She had some demons, your momma, but far as I know, she never confided in anybody. She'd be proud of you, Dirty. We like havin' ya around too." He grinned at Wes, and a huge wave of relief splashed over his system.

He handed Sundance the wrench he was digging around for. "Thanks, I like bein' a Bighorn."

"Doesn't hurt having a pretty little brunette in your bed either, does it?"

"You'd better be talkin' out your ass, Dirty." The voice belonged to Druid, who was suddenly standing near them.

The skin on Wes's neck prickled and he stood to his full height. *Here we go.*

Several people nearby stopped talking and joking to look on. Sundance stood.

"Seems like you take a peculiar interest in who comes to my bed, Druid. Why don't you tell me why." Wes stared down the other biker.

"You keep away from my daughter," the man bit off.

"Did you think sending that woman to my bed would make me give up Stormy? Because all it did was pull us together more."

Druid's already red eyes grew more bloodshot.

"You motherfucker."

Wes had always known Druid was a bottle of C-4 with a short fuse, and he was ready when the man launched himself at him.

Fists hit him in the chest with bruising strength that knocked Wes back a few steps, but he came back at his opponent with double the rage. When he caught Druid around the middle, a scream sounded.

No scream like that came from a biker. Wes had heard that voice enough to know it was Stormy.

"Take it outside! Watch the bikes!" Sundance bellowed.

Druid twisted Wes's shirt front and shoved him against the wall hard enough to crumple a lesser man. But Wes just gave him a grin and came at him harder.

"Asshole, if you fuck up my bike—" One guy's threats were cut off as Wes and Druid danced through the gap. Wes's boot caught the side of a toolbox and the clatter of metal on concrete echoed through the big building.

"Get the fuck outta here, guys!" another biker yelled.

Druid took a swing at Wes, and he ducked the blow.

"Stop! What is wrong with you?" Stormy appeared next to them, hair long and loose and her face flushed pink with anger.

Wes could only see the pink in her cheeks as arousal, though, and he fought all the harder. His right jab rocked Druid's head back.

"Get out!" Two guys bodily removed them from the building. Wes's grin widened. Out here, he could do some real damage to the man who'd been getting under his skin for too long.

With a roar, Wes laid into Druid. They hit the ground, hitting hard enough to send pain shooting through Wes's shoulder. He rolled to his knees and cocked his fist.

Stormy wrapped both her hands around his biceps, her restraint like a fly to a bull. But he stopped dead, too afraid to hurt her.

"Get back, Stormy. Your dad and I have something to settle."

Druid's eyes gleamed a split second before he sent a hard kick at Wes's thigh. Narrowly missing his junk, and damn that fucking hurt. The bruise started welling before Wes could shake off Stormy and beat Druid to a pulp.

Guys circled them and ladies poured out of the club to watch, leaving him and Druid pounding the shit out of each other like the opening act in a violent three-ring circus.

"Motherfucker." Wes spat a glob of blood onto the ground.

"Look at the tough guy—he bleeds like the rest of the world." Druid danced aside, but Wes swept his leg out from under him. He went down with a groan and Wes gave him a punch to the kidney that would have him pissing blood for a week.

"Enough! Stop!" Stormy threw herself between them, and both fell still, panting from exertion and anger.

Wes and Druid reached for her at the same time, and Wes saw red. He picked up the curvy woman, set her on her feet a few steps away and went after Druid for one final round. Determined to end this score and let the man know he no longer held any sway over Stormy. She was a woman, she'd made her choice, and that was Wes.

* * * * *

"Damn fools," Stormy said under her breath as she watched two grown men beat the hell out of each other. Neither seemed to be tiring and they seemed too indestructible to even bleed either. Besides a few drops, it looked like they could go on all day.

Stormy's brother had been interested in dog fights and dragged her with him a time or two. The only thing that would split the beasts up was a startling noise.

Inspiration struck. "Sundance, give me your sidearm."

He looked at her like she'd lost her mind. Then his expression changed. "I won't give it to you, but I'll do the honors." He slipped a hand inside his cut and

119

came out with his Glock. "Cover your pretty ears, ladies," he said and pointed the weapon at the open yard that sprawled toward the mountain range.

The report reached through Stormy's fingers pasted over her ears and did exactly what it was meant to—the guys fell apart.

Her dad planted his hands on his knees, bent over gasping. Wes shook his hands, which had to be swelling from all the blows he'd delivered.

"Don't stand for fighting amongst ourselves," Sundance said, still holding his weapon. "You've proved you're both tough as fucking steel and can't take each other down. The beef between you is officially settled."

Her father cast Sundance a look and then shifted his gaze to Stormy. She grimaced at the rising lump on his browbone.

"Don't even fucking look at her," Dirty bit off.

"Dirty," Sundance barked. "I said stand down. Now, that's her father. He's not goin' anywhere, so make peace or make your own way."

Neither man looked willing to shake hands, and for a minute Stormy feared they'd lay into each other again. But Dirty stepped up to Druid and extended a big hand.

Her dad straightened and stared at it as if it was a bit of roadkill. "Fine," he said and shook.

Their grip looked like a stranglehold, but they parted.

Silence fell over the whole group. Finally, DeeDee broke it. "Lunch is on. Handmade pizza crust."

Everyone headed toward the clubhouse, but Stormy didn't move. Watching what the two fighters would do.

"You okay, Stormy?" her father asked.

She swung on him. "Now that you ask… No. You planted Kylie in Dirty's bed to make him stay away from me, didn't you?"

He stared at her, and she thought of all the times he'd protected her in her lifetime. Too many to count. But Dirty was one thing she didn't need protection from.

She stepped up to her father. "You know I love you, but this fight ends here. Dirty is in my life, and you're going to have to accept it. I can make my own decisions. Even if that's leaving the Bighorns."

Her father's eyes widened in shock. "You'd let him take you away from here? From the family that loves you?"

"I love them too. I love all of you. But lately I've been thinking there's something more out there for me. And you can send a dozen girls to Dirty's bed to make it look like he's cheating, but it won't change my mind about being with him."

He gazed at her for a long minute as if seeing her for the first time. Maybe he was. She'd never stood up to him this way before. Finally, he turned and headed into the club too, leaving her and Dirty in the yard.

"I'm sorry about that," he said quietly, inspecting a swollen knuckle.

She reached for his hand, his big palm like a paw in her own as she checked for broken fingers. Everything looked intact. The man was trained to fight.

She met his stare, a tumultuous gray like a hurricane sea. "You're not coming inside, are you?"

He didn't say anything at first, only searched her face. The kiss of his eyes was like a caress to her soul, but it broke her at the same time.

"I'm gonna go, baby."

"Where?" Her throat closed with emotion. Would she see him again?

"Look, there are things I haven't explained to you. I don't know why I haven't, except I keep a lot to myself."

She waited, heart fluttering at the thought of losing him.

"There are questions about my real mother and father that I've avoided for a lifetime, but it's time I learn the truth. My..." He trailed off and took a step closer to her, palming her cheek.

She leaned into his touch. "Go on," she urged. What she wouldn't give to unburden her soul and if she could give that to Dirty, she'd have a measure of peace after he left.

"My mother and my aunt were sisters. But I share my eyes with my cousins."

She gave a light shake of her head. "That's normal, right? Family traits passed down."

"And also my uncle," he said flatly.

Her heart gave a flip-flop at the torment on his rugged face. "You think your uncle's your real father?"

He dropped his hand from her face and shoved his fingers through his hair. "I don't know. I don't know what to think. But I have to find out."

She stepped closer and put her arms around him. Going on tiptoe to mold her body to his, hating that she wasn't strong enough to keep from shaking.

He made a noise in his chest and pulled her tight to his big body. They stood that way for a long minute. "I'll be back, baby."

All she could do was believe him. At least until he betrayed that trust. She stepped back.

"I'll be here, Dirty." She didn't add *waiting*, though it was on the tip of her tongue.

"I'd kiss you but then I won't stop."

"I understand." She did. He had to fight his demons to come back to her whole. Then maybe they could continue their life together, make their own way with or without the Bighorns in their lives.

She smiled and he returned it, gray eyes twinkling. "See ya soon, Dirty."

With that, she walked into the clubhouse, feeling his stare on her back and burning to run back into his arms.

But she resisted.

A few minutes later, she heard the engine of his Harley and knew he was gone.

The clubhouse was full of talk about the fight, but her dad was sitting apart from them. As soon as she entered, he walked up to her and handed her a bottle of beer. "Thought you could use this."

"Thanks."

He stared at her too closely.

She twisted off the cap and raised the bottle to her lips. The cold brew was tasteless in her mouth.

Her dad rested a hand on her shoulder. "He'll be back."

"Why do you care? You just tried to break his neck."

A huff of laughter left him. "Tried is the operative word." He skimmed his fingers over his bruised brow with a grimace. "At least I found out what I needed to."

Her gaze shot to his. "What?"

"That he's worthy of keeping you safe."

Chapter Seven

Pulling into Eagle Crest on his bike felt surreal. The ranch felt like another world.

One where he could roam free and sweat out his frustrations through hard work. Many a time he'd come home after running down a difficult fugitive solely to work it out of his system.

This time, he felt weighted with worry, though. He was determined get to the bottom of why his mother had run away and left him behind. This time he wasn't buying the answer he always got—that his momma knew he'd have a solid home with them.

And it was high time to find out if he wasn't a Roshannon in name only.

A couple dogs burst around the barn and headed for his bike as he rolled up the driveway and stopped in front of the house. He spoke a word to them and they settled at his familiar voice.

He cut the engine and pushed the kickstand into place with his heel before climbing off. The dogs leaped at him, barking with enthusiasm now. Chuckling, he bent to scratch their ears and one offered his butt.

Laughing now, Wes gave them a spot of attention before looking to the house and then the fields... He looked beyond to the cattle dotting the land and dragged in a deep breath of air. *Home.*

No matter where he fit in or who he actually was, Eagle Crest would always be his home. Years ago, he'd thought about giving up hunting bail-jumpers one day and taking over the ranch with Uncle Matthias.

Now, he didn't know.

Throwing a look at the other vehicles in the drive, he stepped onto the porch. Wasn't so rare for his cousins to be home on a weekend — they often tried to gather at least once a month. But Wes wasn't sure he wanted them around for what he needed to say to his aunt and uncle.

When he opened the door, a baby's wail came to him. He closed the door with a smile — Aiden was a new father. The man was born to boss people around, and now he had one of his own to boss.

Aunt Winter appeared in the mudroom, a dishtowel in hand. Her eyes widened and her jaw dropped. She rushed forward and threw her arms around him.

"Oh my God! Wes, we weren't expecting you. Haven't heard from you in too long. I'm *so* glad you're here!"

He squeezed her and planted a kiss on her cheek. "Hope it's okay I came."

She swatted him with the towel. "Okay? You know we want you home permanently." She stepped back to eye his attire of leather and denim and made a *tsking* sound. She didn't ask him to put on his Stetson, but she didn't need to anyway.

He wanted to. His heart was too full with the sights and smells of Eagle Crest not to truly feel he belonged here.

"What's everyone doing?"

"They all just got here. Oh my, is your jaw bruised?" She pinched his chin as if getting ready to rub away a dirty spot with a thumb.

He pulled back. "I'm fine. Could use a drink though."

She was set in motion with the task. Waving him along, she listed all the contents of the refrigerator. He emerged from the mudroom to see his twin cousins gathered in the living room with their pretty wives and the new baby.

"Look what the hounds dragged in. Thought I heard a bike." Aiden stood and crossed the room in two strides to clap Wes on the back. Judd was there too, a mirror image of his brother and looking happier than he'd ever seen him.

Wes greeted his cousins with genuine affection. Then he turned to their wives. Each beautiful and smiling at him. If he ever brought a wife home, would she fit in with them? He pictured Stormy with these ladies and wasn't sure.

"Who's the newcomer?" He hovered over the baby in Amaryllis's arms. To him, infants all looked like worms, but this one had the Roshannon eyes.

He smiled and was introduced to Sawyer Matthias Roshannon.

"Want to hold him? He's not even stinky." Amaryllis smiled down at her baby the way only a mother does.

"Later." He straightened and met his uncle's eyes. The same as his. And if Wes looked closer, he could pick out other features he shared with his uncle—the thick dark hair and the square jaw, though his uncle's was getting softer with age.

"Like to talk to you and Aunt Winter alone."

Something passed in his uncle's eyes, but he gave a no-nonsense nod.

"What's this? You're conducting Roshannon business without us?" Judd asked.

"This isn't something you should be part of. Yet."

"Hold on." Aunt Winter's face paled and she twisted the dishtowel in her hands. "Wes, is this about the bikers? Are you in trouble?"

"Hell no. I *am* the law, Aunty. Why would I be on the wrong side of it? It's about my mother. And father." He swung his gaze to Matthias, though he couldn't quite meet his stare.

"Whatever's said should be said to all of us. Judd and I have a right to know what's happening in our own family."

"Do we have to do this right now, Wes honey? There's dinner to put on and—" Aunt Winter silenced at Matthias's touch on her shoulder. A look passed between them.

They started toward the kitchen and everybody got up to follow. Wes turned to look at his cousins. He supposed it was their business too—finally hearing whether or not the rumors they'd endured as kids and into adulthood about being brothers and not cousins were true.

* * * * *

Seated in his usual spot around the farmhouse table, about to confront his relatives about his true identity, was one of the more nerve-wracking moments of Wes's life. He could do with a beer right now and realized with surprise how much the Bighorns had really rubbed off on him.

He wasn't the same boy who'd left Eagle Crest. His career had taken him places and now he was coming back to find his roots.

His aunt and uncle sat at the head of the table, hands interlocked. United as always.

Wes drew a deep breath and held it till his lungs burned. When he released it, the words flowed out as if he'd rehearsed them.

"I think you know what I want to discuss."

The barest of nods from Matthias.

"I checked some DNA a while back."

Judd's head snapped up. Aunt Winter's face paled alarmingly.

"I went to the Bighorns thinking I'd find the man who fathered me there. I took a sample of his DNA and Judd ran it for me."

Everyone looked to Judd.

"It didn't match," Wes continued. He eyed Matthias. "I could go deeper into my suspicions—I have all the resources at my fingertips—but I believe you kept it hidden from me and the rest of the world for a reason."

Judd and Aiden exchanged glances. Their wives' eyes were wide and even the baby was quiet, the pacifier bobbing in his mouth as he drifted off.

"So, I'm coming to you and Aunt Winter for the real answers about my mom and how I ended up a Roshannon—a real Roshannon by blood." He held his breath. There—he'd said it. And nobody was arguing his point.

Yet.

Aiden made a sharp movement and Aunt Winter's face crumpled for a split second before she regained composure and smoothed it over.

Judd spoke up. "Wes, you're talking crazy. I never believed you were in harm's way with the bikers, but it seems they've scrambled your brains."

Wes gave a shake of his head. "Ask yourselves why I look like you—and you resemble your father more than my mother's sister." He nodded to his aunt.

She moved to stand and leave the table, but Matthias kept her hand in his hold and drew her back down. "Time we talk to these boys like the men they are," he said softly.

"What the fuck is going on?" Aiden asked.

"I really am your son, aren't I?" Wes stared into Matthias's eyes, so like his own.

He squeezed his wife's hand and squared his shoulders. This was where they'd all gotten their grit—from this man.

A man who was Wes's father too. Why had he been denied all these years the right to call him Dad, Daddy, Pa, Pops?

"It's my fault we kept this secret from you so long," Aunt Winter blurted.

"Jesus, Mom," Judd croaked out, and Cecily wrapped an arm around him.

"It was a decision made by both of us. It's a difficult thing to explain to children, adults or strangers. People wouldn't have understood, and you boys would have spent your lives explaining where you fit into a family tree." Matthias stared into Wes's eyes—his soul.

"I *am* your father, son. And I raised you with the same love as I raised the twins. I hope I did right by you in that sense."

Wes couldn't speak or even nod. The tears lay hot behind his eyes and he didn't dare blink.

"Holy fuck," Aiden breathed. "How?"

Aunt Winter issued a shaky breath. "Your father and I got together and then decided to part ways early in our relationship. It was only months we dated, but when I left the area to pursue a different life, I was pregnant and didn't yet know it." She twisted her hands into a knot and stared at her fingers.

"Had I known, I would have dragged your momma back immediately and married her. But she'd made it clear we were over, and well, a few months later, Winter's sister Blanche ran into me sitting alone at a restaurant. She joined me, one thing led to another and…"

Aiden shoved away from the table and jammed his hands into his hair as he paced away. Wes ignored him. His suspicions were confirmed—Matthias had slept with both sisters and gotten them pregnant within months of each other. Now he wanted to get to the part where his mother gave him up and left for good.

His worst fear was hearing this couple had driven her off. But that went against everything he knew about his family and the morals ingrained in him from birth.

"Go on," he managed to say, voice gritty.

"Blanche and I weren't really a thing—just offering comfort I think. The loss of Winter was hard on both of us. Well, then Winter returned pregnant and I pretty much married her on the spot. Then Blanche came to us in the family way."

Aiden walked back to the table and dropped into his seat. "And then what? You offered to take the baby," he gestured at Wes, who was the six-two, two-hundred-pound version of that coupling, "and sent his momma on her way?"

"No." Aunt Winter shook her head. "Blanche wasn't really the motherly type and she wanted to abort." She winced again as she settled her gaze on Wes. Her eyes flooded and tears streamed down her cheeks. "We've loved you like our own, Wes. We named you on the day you were born and gave you the Roshannon name, as it should be. But what we did in keeping this hidden from you all was solely to make things easier on you. To protect you from gossip."

Judd lowered his face into his hands and made a harsh noise. Then he raised his head and stared at Wes, throat working. "I always wanted you to be a real brother, Wes. And now I've got it." He shoved back from the table and Wes stood to meet him.

Judd and Aiden wrapped him in a rough hug while the ladies in the room quietly cried. Wes felt strangely elated, the relief dizzying.

When they broke apart, Matthias—his father—was there to wrap him in a stronghold. That's when Wes's tears flowed and he couldn't hold back any longer, especially when his aunt joined in the embrace.

* * * * *

133

Saddling horses was always a soothing chore for Wes. He took pride in ensuring the mounts were comfortable and well-treated. While he tightened the strap on the big gelding for the long ride out to the mountains to drive back the herd, he double-checked the way the tack fit.

When he straightened, Aiden was swinging into his own saddle, heels to flanks.

"Get a move on, bro," he tossed over his shoulder along with a grin.

Wes's face split into a smile and he swung his leg up and over his mount. A click of his tongue and they were in motion. Judd was farther ahead, riding along with some of the ranch hands who helped them move the cattle on a weekly basis. His uncle — *dad* — always said that the secret to good cattle farming was in the grazing land and to move often.

Wes hung back to look at the scenery — fields running right up to the base of the mountains, snow-capped in the distance. The Bighorns club was right over that range... and Stormy.

He always missed her when one of them left, but this time it felt like a bone-deep ache. She was in his blood, and he didn't exactly know what to do about it.

Aiden dropped back until he was alongside Wes. "You still thinkin' on last night's revelations?"

Wes shrugged. "Little bit. Hard not to wonder if anything would have been different if I'd been raised as a brother. But prob'ly not."

"Yeah, prob'ly not."

He considered talking to Aiden about Stormy. They'd shared a few stories of females over the years. Hell, they'd shared a woman—Aiden's ex, but just that once. Still, that was a long time ago, and Wes wasn't into that sort of thing anymore.

"Speak your mind, Wes. I know you've got something weighin' on it. Is it a fugitive?"

"Nah, not job-related."

"So it's female."

"Well, it isn't animal, vegetable or mineral."

Aiden grinned at the reference to the game they played as kids, trying to guess what the person was thinking of.

Wes nodded, moving with the horse's strides. It felt good to be out in the open this way. "Yeah, a woman. She's in the club."

"Does that mean...?" Aiden arched a brow.

"No, not that kind of club girl. She's different." *And I think I'm in love with her.*

He didn't say the last part.

"Well, if you're gonna bring her home to meet the family, now's the time to do it. Strike while they're all sympathetic from last night's talk."

Wes chuckled and flicked the reins to make his lazy mount to keep pace with Aiden's. "I wouldn't do that."

"What—bring her home to Eagle Crest or take advantage of the situation? You realize what my mom did to me and Judd with our wives, right?"

Wes nodded. She'd picked at her sons until they'd told her to stay out of their business, but she meant well. He wasn't sure if she'd do that with him or not. She *had* said she'd felt the same love for him as the twins.

"I'll keep it in mind."

"How long you stayin' this time?" Aiden looked as if he already knew the answer.

"Movin' out tonight. I've got business to see to."

"The woman."

He rode in silence a moment. "Her dad's trying to push me out of her life."

"I suppose it's not good manners to kick his ass."

Wes grunted. "I tried."

"Wait—tried? I've never seen a guy you can't take down, Wes." Aiden tugged his hat brim, a habit he'd had since he was a kid.

"He's tough as nails."

"Want me to run him? Give me his details."

"Nah, it's okay. Not a threat, just a hindrance. He seems to be in Stormy's business too much."

"Stormy."

136

"Yeah."

"My offer stands—I'll run interference with Momma so you can bring Stormy home."

"Well, you could tell her you're ready to start working on Roshannon Baby Number Two. That'd keep her occupied."

Aiden waggled his brows. "Ya never know."

Chapter Eight

Stormy picked at the food on her plate, one of her favorite dishes of tacos made with love by her dear friend DeeDee. But she had no appetite—at least not for food.

"You're going to waste away. A man likes a woman with some meat on her hips." DeeDee smiled around her own bite of soft taco stuffed with all the fixin's.

Pushing back, Stormy said, "The food's great. Thanks, DeeDee. But I'm not that hungry."

"Uh-oh."

She blinked. "What?"

Beyond the kitchen windows, bikes gathered, but the sound of engines as the guys revved up for another ride made the glass panes shudder.

"You couldn't be pregnant, could you?" DeeDee's eyes were as round as an owl's.

Stormy picked up a taco and took a big bite. "Definitely not."

"You're certain? You and Dirty—"

"Are safe," she said firmly. "Condoms and I have the IUD. Almost foolproof."

"Okay, but things happen."

"I know, but not this time."

"So if it's not a baby, it has to be heartache." DeeDee polished off her food.

Stormy remained silent.

"About that heartache—" DeeDee started.

The cry came from the front room. "Dirty! Holy crap, you look good, babe."

Stormy rocketed out of her chair at the sweet butt's high-pitched squeal and ran out of the kitchen.

There he was, big and leather-clad and windblown. His gaze landed on her—warm, heavy. Making her delirious with desire after one long look.

She couldn't draw a deep breath.

He ignored the girls fawning over him, and in five steps grabbed Stormy and pulled her off her feet.

She threw her arms around him to the cheers of DeeDee behind her as Dirty strode down the hall to his room. The door barely slammed shut before he crushed his lips to hers. Tasting like the same dark lust he always did except with a new hint of spring grasses.

Dragging his head down, she parted her lips for him. His tongue sank deep, claiming her as wholly as his cock surely would just as soon as they could get their clothes off.

She moaned as he rocked his erection into her.

"That better all be for me."

"Oh, it is, baby." He lifted his head long enough to pierce her with his gaze. "I've been wanting you since the moment I drove down that mountain."

"I wanted you more." Her breathy admission made his eyes warm. He grabbed her leg and pulled it high on his hip to angle his cock straight at her pussy. Even with denim between them, he had her hot and panting in seconds.

"Take off your clothes," he ordered, releasing her.

She stepped back and went for the hem of her top, pulling it overhead and tossing it aside. Her hair floated down around her back, and his gaze followed it.

Feeling empowered with his expression of want, she stripped off the rest of her clothes slowly. Taking her time to build up to the finale they both wanted so badly. She'd been burning for this man, and while he was gone had realized more than ever that she loved him.

She dropped her bra, and he fisted his hands at his sides. He looked damn good, just like the sweet butt had said. All chiseled man with low-slung jeans and his leather jacket collar brushing his too-long hair on his nape.

He bore a scratch on his cheekbone. That was new.

"You get into a fight?"

The corner of his lips turned up. "With an ornery goat. Didn't want me to pick him up and haul him away from his harem."

"A goat?" She unbuttoned her jeans and unzipped her fly.

He wet his lips and nodded. "He thinks it's his job to impregnate all the females on the ranch. Had to separate them before we end up with ninety kids."

She issued a puff of a laugh as she pushed her jeans over her hips. His gaze latched onto the black panties she wore. Her stomach dropped out with excitement as she stripped those down too.

"Fuck, you're gorgeous."

She kicked off her garments and stood nude before him.

"Cup your breasts for me."

A trickle of warmth between her thighs had her squirming as she cradled her breasts in her hands.

"Run your thumbs over those pink nipples. Fuck yeah." His voice came out as a growl, but he didn't move to step closer.

A shiver of pleasure rocked her on her bare feet.

"Now slide your hands down your body."

She did his bidding, her breath coming in quick pants. When she reached her bikini line, he flashed his gaze to hers.

"Now spread apart your pussy lips so I can see how wet you are."

Oh my God.

Five minutes before she'd been sitting in the kitchen wanting him and now she stood before him taking his every… dirty… command.

Need blossomed in her lower belly as she pressed her pussy lips. The cooler air hit her soaking folds and fresh juices slipped out to dampen her inner thighs.

"Fuck, I missed you. Get on the bed and spread those legs wide for me, baby. I'm going to tongue-fuck you until you can't remember your name."

She already couldn't as she stepped backward to stretch out on his bed.

He stripped off his leather jacket with precise movements of a man who gave great attention to everything he did. He was no different in bed, taking his time, drawing sounds and feelings from her that she hadn't realized possible.

He set aside his jacket and cut and then his T-shirt. He kicked off his boots but kept on the jeans.

With lidded eyes, he climbed onto the bed and hovered over her. The brush of denim against her sensitive thighs made her suck in sharply. He planted a hand on her breast as he leaned in and kissed her.

Thoroughly.

Completely.

She clung to him, giving back as good as he gave. When he pulled away and slid down her body, hooking her thighs over his shoulders, she stopped breathing.

The first touch of his hot tongue dragged a cry from her. He pressed the flat of his tongue against her seam, soaking up the juices.

"Oh my God. Dirty, lick me. I need to come."

He rumbled a response and eased his tongue up and down her pussy, swirling around her clit and then through her folds to her opening. He sank his tongue deep and then flicked it shallowly until she strained for more.

She twisted her hands in the covers and trembled on the verge of something so huge, so much bigger than her.

This loving was new to her, but she had a feeling most people didn't feel this way. Never found someone worthy of the emotion.

He danced his tongue over her pussy, and she couldn't remain quiet.

Plunging in again, he set her on fire. Stroking her to a frenzy with his lips and tongue and then when she was on the verge of coming, added two fingers.

She clenched around those callused digits, back bowing off the bed as her release shook her. Waves of ecstasy stole every thought from her mind and she only knew Dirty. His lips, his tongue, fingers, eyes. God, those eyes…

A hiccupping breath left her, and he gave her a satisfied smile from his perch between her legs.

"Get inside me. I need you — now."

"Look who's giving commands." He pushed onto his knees and with a flick of his wrist, unbuttoned his jeans. Veins snaked down his arm to his hand. Suddenly, she wanted to lick every inch of him and learn the contour of those veins and each muscle on his body.

He paused, fly hanging open, the bulge of his cock harnessed by black cotton boxer briefs.

"I did some thinking while I was away, Stormy."

Her mind barely rolled with the conversation. "About what?"

"I want to make one thing clear between us."

Her heart raced. "What's that?" she whispered.

He cupped his bulge and stared down at her. "You belong to me. There won't be any other women. And you won't have any other men."

Her heart flipped over and took off at a higher pace. "You're asking me to be exclusive?"

"Yeah." He drew his thick length from his jeans and wrapped his long fingers around it.

She beckoned to him. "Come here. Get inside me."

"Without a condom?"

"I'm on birth control and I haven't been with anyone else. You?"

He didn't hesitate to flatten himself against her, the tip of his swollen cock poised at her entrance.

Looking into her eyes, he gave one shove and filled her completely.

"I'm clean, baby." He began to move. Slow strokes that built a heat in her that she couldn't control. Just when she thought she'd have to beg, he jerked his hips faster and faster until she split apart, contracting around his cock for too many seconds to count.

When she came up for air, he was staring at her. Something in his eyes sent a warm feeling through her entire body. "That's one. Now come for me again."

He rolled her over and settled her atop him. Straddling his big body, she gave him a flirty smile. "I can torment you the way you torment me."

"You already are." He pushed upward, sending the tip of his cock brushing against her innermost point. She cried out, head dropping back.

He bundled her hair in his fist and urged her to move. Watching her face as she came apart for him a second time.

She collapsed on his broad chest, panting. "You either have the control of a saint or you don't want me very much."

"Oh, I want you. I want every part of you." He cupped her breasts, thumbing her nipples as he kept her flattened to him and rocked his hips in a rhythm that sent her shooting upward all over again.

The man must have been an exotic dancer in another lifetime, the way he moved those hips. She kissed him with all the passion oozing through her body and he gave it right back.

Exclusive. She couldn't stop thinking about him being her man.

He gripped her ass, dragging her down on his cock with sharper thrusts. He seemed to stretch inside her and she knew he was close. His eyes darkened to coal-black.

"You want me to come inside you, baby? I'm so fucking close."

A thrill hit her. The thought of him spilling inside her made her move faster, once more on the verge of orgasm.

"Yesss," she moaned, throwing herself into moving in a way that would force all the control out of his body.

He clenched his jaw, his eyes fixed shut. She rotated her hips three more times... four. Then she came with a cry and felt the first hot splash of him inside her.

* * * * *

Yeah, Wes's intelligence was questionable. What had he been thinking to ask Stormy to give herself to him and him alone? He wasn't in any position to bind her to him, not with his job and secrets hanging over his head.

Now the object of his desire was tucked snugly against his side, sweat-damp from their coupling.

"Tell me... about the goats." Her voice was sleepy, though he felt the energy pumping through her frame.

He chuckled and looked down at her. Sweeping aside the hair from her eyes. "My un—" he stopped and corrected himself "—my father's ranch. And goats."

She pushed onto one elbow to gaze at him. "So you found out the truth."

He nodded.

"You were raised thinking he was your uncle when really he's your dad?"

"That's right. Sounds more like a soap opera than it really is living it. After the initial news was out in the open, nothing had really changed."

"Not even in here?" She tapped a forefinger on his chest.

"No. I've always loved them like parents and my cousins as brothers."

She nodded as if she understood. Peace settled over him.

"Where is everyone?" he asked.

"Rode out with the Green Hills guys. They'll be back in time to eat the pig roasting on the spit."

He tensed. "I missed riding to meet them."

"Yeah. It's okay. They'll understand. You'll meet them when they return."

"Or…" He looked down into her eyes. "We could catch up."

She poked his chest. "You've got balls, thinking to flaunt me on the back of your bike in front of my dad."

He threw her a crooked grin and rolled out of bed to his feet. He tossed her the pile of clothes she'd stripped off. "Get dressed and put on your leather. We've gotta put some speed on to catch up."

Within minutes Wes had his bike revving and Stormy's thighs were wrapped around his hips. She held on tight to his middle, her cheek against his shoulder. The freedom of being in the open air with the only woman he wanted in his universe made his chest ache with sweet exhilaration.

Ahead of them on the curving mountain road, an elk crossed the asphalt, in no hurry. The grace and beauty made Wes smile. This was what life on the open road was all about.

"That was freakin' amazing," Stormy said in his ear.

He nodded and covered her hand where it wrapped his middle. For miles he kept the pace steady, but when they began to wind their way out of the mountains, he kicked it into gear.

She squealed and held on tighter. He couldn't quit grinning.

When they spotted the bike formation ahead, Stormy let out a cheer.

"Hold on," he said over his shoulder and gunned it.

* * * * *

Stormy walked up to Dirty and wrapped her arm around his middle. His muscles were warm under his leather, flexing as he drew her near. He held a half-finished beer in the other hand, using it to gesture as he spoke with the Green Hills member.

Loud music echoed through the yard, and the party was in various states of digression. The liquor was flowing freely and the Bighorns were definitely getting their party on.

Stormy wanted to get Dirty away, though. She wanted to talk to him about what had been weighing on her mind since he'd told her about Eagle Crest. She wanted to bring up the topic of him taking her home with him, but how?

She was always a straight-shooter, never holding back what she wanted to voice. But it was a big step for both of them. She'd be walking away from the club family for a time and maybe Wes wasn't ready to introduce her to his people.

Patiently, she waited for him to finish talking to the Green Hills member. Then she went on tiptoe to whisper into his ear. "Can I speak with you alone?"

His gray eyes zeroed in on her and a worry line appeared between his brows. "Sure."

She took his hand and led him through groups of people seated around a bonfire and many more standing around drinking and BS-ing. When they reached a picnic table, she pointed to it.

He nodded and sank to the bench. She stood before him, too nervous to sit. When he took her by the hands and looked up at her, she saw she was worrying him more than necessary. She just needed to spit it out.

"Dirty, I've been thinking about those horses you talked about on your family's ranch."

His brows shot up. "What about them?"

"I... I'd like to see them."

A beat of silence. His warm fingers enveloping hers. "You're asking me to take you to Eagle Crest?"

She nodded. "I mean, you don't have to if you don't want or you're not ready. I just..."

He yanked her down across his thighs and lightly dug his fingers into her sides, tickling her. She giggled and squirmed to get away. "You had me worried as hell and you asked to see my horses?"

"Stop!" She cried at his ruthless tickling. "Yes, that's all I wanted. Now stop!"

He did, cupping her face in one big hand and looking deeply into her eyes. "Your father won't like it."

She waved a hand. "Oh, who cares about him? He hasn't tried to break your legs all night."

"That's true. Maybe he's changed his thinking about me."

"I hope so. It helps having my brother around to distract him."

Dirty went still. "Brother?"

"Yeah, you haven't met him. He hasn't been around much, but he came with the Green Hills guys."

Dirty looked around.

"He isn't here. As soon as I find him, I'll introduce you, though. Now..." She moved his hand upward, the darkness covering the fact that she placed his hand over her breast. Her breaths came faster as she felt the heat of his hand seep through her top and harden the tip of her nipple. She couldn't get enough of Dirty and now their relationship was moving in a direction she couldn't help but feel a thrill over.

She tipped her face up for his kiss and wasn't disappointed when he settled his lips over hers, claiming each quiet moan for his own.

Chapter Nine

Stormy woke next to Dirty, but the first thing that struck her wasn't the odor of smoke and booze—it was eggs.

Frying eggs. And bacon.

Her stomach growled, and she wondered how the heck she could be hungry. In the past two days since coming to Eagle Crest with Dirty, she'd eaten more than she did in a week's time.

Dirty said his Aunt Winter loved to keep him and his brothers full to overflowing and there was no point in Stormy trying to fight it. But she didn't want to step foot on a scale when she got home.

She moaned as the delicious scents teased her nostrils. "Is that oranges I smell?"

Dirty's chest rumbled against her back. "Yes, Aunt Winter will be squeezing them for juice."

"Mm. Hand-squeezing?"

His laugh shook her again. "No, she has a juicer. Used to do it by hand, though, until we chipped in and got her a juicer when we were in high school."

"It's so early. I can't get used to these early mornings."

"That's because we're up till dawn in the club. Want to sleep in and I'll tell Aunt Winter to save you a plate?"

"No. I'll get up with you. I don't want to miss anything you do."

First thing, Dirty had taken her to the paddock and let her pick out a horse. She'd spent a lot of time crooning to them and petting them, but it was soon evident that one favored her. And that was the one Stormy'd been riding for the past two days.

She had to admit, her riding skills were rusty, but luckily, she had a sexy cowboy instructor.

Dirty was scorching hot in black leather. But put him in worn Wranglers, a T-shirt and a cowboy hat and just the sight of him made her feel she was about to combust.

He wrapped his thick arm around her waist and tugged her closer to his bare body. Her ass pressed against something hard.

"Umm, good morning?"

"Mm-hmm." He nuzzled her neck.

She loved this about him—the way he spoke in hums and grunts of pleasure in the mornings. In two short days she'd been at Eagle Crest with him, she'd learned more about him than in months spent at the club.

He slid his hand along her rib cage until he cradled her breast in his palm. She issued a soft sight of happiness. Being in his arms had always thrilled her, but this was a whole new level of their relationship. Did he feel it too?

She felt more relaxed than she had in a very long time.

A faint clang of a frying pan and lid colliding signaled breakfast was served.

"I'm going to have to diet for a year to get these pounds off me."

He rocked his hips again. "I can come up with some exercise."

She slapped at him and another clank from downstairs had Dirty rolling out of bed and Stormy following.

As Dirty pulled on a fresh pair of boxer briefs and jeans, he shot her one of those crooked smiles that sent tingles racing through her lower belly. He pulled on a white T-shirt and looked ready to tackle the day while she felt like a mess.

"I need an extra minute or two." She threw on a robe, gathered her clothes and slipped out of the room. In the bathroom, she grabbed toothbrush and toothpaste, watching her reflection as she brushed and washed her face, added a bit of lip balm and sunscreen. Finally, she dressed and pulled her hair back into a loose ponytail at her nape.

The woman looking back at her was not one she recognized. Not because she didn't look the same. But because she was different inside.

She looked like a woman in love.

This woman had brighter eyes, a fresh glow to her face and a smile that wouldn't stop toying with the corners of her lips.

She bundled her robe in her arms and when she opened the door, Dirty was leaning against the frame, gray eyes burning down at her.

"Sorry I took so long. You need to brush your teeth, huh?"

"You look beautiful. It was worth the wait." He brushed his knuckles over her cheekbone and she caught his hand, squeezing.

"Thank you for bringing me here, Dirty."

Another clang of pan and lid announced his aunt was getting impatient.

"Better hurry," he said.

"I'll go down and see if she needs any help." On her way to the stairs, she paused to toss her robe onto the bed they shared. The big queen-sized bed of his youth, as he obviously couldn't have fit in anything smaller.

The ranch house was decorated with a simple style of country quilts and the occasional wooden cutout rooster standing sentry on a shelf. But the photos of the family were what really made the space homey.

Dirty and his brothers growing throughout the years. Wet and wrapped in towels along a river. A graduation ceremony, with Dirty's cap cocked on his head in complete defiance of convention.

She smiled at the photographs recording him growing up along with his brothers and looked forward to meeting them, though it would surely rattle her nerves at first.

Her restless feelings at the club had vanished, leaving only pure happiness here on the ranch. It was everything she'd hoped for and more. And it made her realize she wanted...

Well, this.

A comfortable home, fresh air. And plenty of loving.

"We—" Winter came around the corner and swallowed whatever she was about to say when she spotted Stormy.

"Hi." She smiled. "Dirty's not down yet. He's brushing his teeth."

"Ah. Come along and sit down to breakfast then. Matthias has already tucked in—you'd think he's a teenager with the way he packs away the food. We—Dirty will be lucky to get a crumb."

"Then I'd better beat him to the table." She followed Winter into the eat-in kitchen and took a seat at the round table standing before a big double window with a checked green and white valance. The steaming bowls of food had been covered with lids to keep everything warm, but the delicious scents seeped out.

"Oh the orange juice." She picked up the pitcher and poured a tall glass, moaning as she brought it to her lips and tasted the bright citrus.

"You like it, dear?" Winter beamed.

Dirty dropped into the seat next to her and offered a crooked grin to the people who'd raised him. "She could smell it from upstairs."

"It's delicious. Thank you." With the orangey goodness in her belly, she filled her plate with scrambled eggs, bacon and hash browns.

Dirty fought her over the last slice of bacon, but she gave it up to him in the end.

"I can fry more if you'd like," Winter offered, half-rising from her seat.

"No, this is fine. I'm used to eating very little in the mornings."

Winter eyed him. She'd done this a few times in Stormy's presence, and she wasn't sure what to make of the long looks. It was a mixture of pride, worry and something else. As if she wanted to say something but held back.

Dirty had told Stormy that his aunt didn't approve of him joining the Bighorns, so maybe that was it. But Stormy couldn't help but wonder what would be said, and if it might be her own presence stopping Winter from speaking her mind.

Later she'd try to give the two some time alone.

Matthias and Dirty talked ranch life—separating certain cows who'd calf soon. Keeping the bull away from others that weren't ready yet.

When Winter asked her if she wanted to help with the chickens after breakfast, she nodded with a smile. "I'd love that. Though I have no clue what to do."

"It's easy. I'll show you the ways. Then maybe we can have some girl-talk."

At her elbow, Dirty tensed. She swung her gaze to him and found his jaw clenched around a bite of food, the muscle flickering wildly, like a ticking bomb.

He didn't want her alone with his aunt? Why would that be?

"I was taking Stormy out with me to tend the herd," he said, fork poised over his plate. His big hand dwarfed the silverware.

Was it her or was Winter's smile too wide, too accommodating?

"Of course. If that's what you want, dear. I'm not a slave driver, forcing you to help with the chickens."

Suddenly, she wanted to know what the woman had to say to her. Under the table, she rested a hand on Dirty's muscled thigh. *I'll be okay. I can hold my own.*

She *had* been raised a Bighorn, after all.

"I'd love to help with the chickens." She squeezed Dirty's thigh and felt his hand come down atop hers, the weight warm and comforting.

Breakfast talk went on. A meeting of the cattle ranchers guild was mentioned for later in the week.

"You two should come along. You know it's more of a party than a real meeting," Winter said, looking between them.

Dirty gave Stormy a long look that said he'd welcome having the house to themselves more than any party.

"We'll see." Dirty's voice grated out as he squeezed her thigh.

He pushed back from the table and Matthias stood too. "Meet ya in the yard," he said to Dirty.

He gave a hard nod. "You want to come along or help with the chickens?" He slid his gaze to his aunt. Something passed between them, something that seemed to vibrate like Morse code running along a line.

"I'll help Winter." Stormy offered a smile and got up to start clearing plates. Dirty dropped a kiss between her brows and went outside.

With the kitchen tidied and the breakfast cleared away, she and Winter dug into Chickens 101. Winter laughed at how little Stormy knew about the animals and joked nobody should be ignorant of what's on their dinner plate. She had to admit, it was a good rule and she threw herself into feeding, watering and cleaning after the flock.

While they worked, a peaceful calm stole over Stormy. One she'd only experienced here on this ranch.

"You know, it's so lovely here. I can't imagine ever being sad while living this kind of life."

Winter beamed at her. "I feel the same, sweetie. I'd never live anywhere else." She eyed Stormy for a long minute. "You love my boy."

A lump lodged in Stormy's throat, though why it was there, she couldn't say. She was happier than she'd ever been. She dropped her gaze to the ground she was raking and nodded.

"He doesn't know," Winter said gently.

"I haven't told him, no."

"Why not? If it's not too forward of me to ask."

She straightened, the rake handle feeling suddenly cold in her hands. "It's complicated."

"Love's rarely easy."

She nodded.

"It's worth figuring out, though. I can't tell you how happy I am to see my sons settled with wives and children of their own. You've seen the wedding photos on the walls, I'm sure."

She bobbed her head. "Beautiful couples."

"I wouldn't mind putting up one of you and Wes as well, sweetie. You'd fit right in. If you stick around, you'll meet everyone else. They come up every few weekends or so..." She continued talking, but Stormy had zoned out.

Zeroed in.

On one name. Wes.

Wes was Dirty, Dirty was Wes. She was in love with a man named Wes.

Her heart warmed as she said it over and over in her mind. Just that tiny kernel of knowledge had done so much to expand that love in her heart.

* * * * *

Wes knelt in the thick grass and braced a gloved hand on the tractor to peer up under it. The scents of oil mixed with crushed grass. He sat back on his haunches and looked at his uncle.

Father.

It was takin' some getting used to, thinking of Matthias as his dad. He wasn't sure why, though. He'd spent an entire year between nine and ten years old pretending it was the case.

Right around the time he'd been bullied in school for being a string bean and "not a real Roshannon."

"Well, son? Is it leakin' or not?"

Wes nodded. This wasn't the first time Matthias had called him son, but the word was charged with electricity that zapped Wes with a warm happiness now.

"Dammit. Another gasket?"

"More'n likely." Wes pushed to his feet and looked back toward the house.

"You don't need to worry about her."

Wes jerked his head toward his father. "What makes you think I am?"

Instead of answering, he asked a question of his own. "Why is it you asked us not to call you by your name?" He cocked a brow in the same way Judd and Aiden did—the same way *he* did.

Wes pushed out a harsh sigh. It had gone against the grain to ask this of his family, but he'd felt it wasn't exactly the time to let Stormy into his entire life. As soon as she heard his name, she'd know who he was.

And how much did she know about this Alexander Bonner? She could be tipped off, thinking Wes had come to the Bighorns under false pretenses.

There was also the niggling question in his mind that Bonner was her brother. Since their talk at the party, that sixth sense was blaring like a fucking fire siren. Something he couldn't ignore.

All he had to do was ask Stormy her last name, but somehow the secrets between them felt big and difficult to conquer. He didn't want to end what they had.

Matthias let out a rough sigh too. "She doesn't know anything about you being a bounty hunter, does she?"

"Nope." He picked at a string on his shirt pocket. "And it's worse — one of my bounties is in the club."

"Damn, you've boxed yourself into a corner, that's for certain. She won't be happy when she learns the truth."

He leaned heavily against the tractor. "No, she won't. I'll probably lose her. But can I ignore a fugitive, not capture him when I know where he's hiding?" He shook his head. "I'm not sure that's in my blood."

His father watched him for a long moment. "Seems like there's more."

He always did know Wes.

"She mentioned a brother, someone I've never seen or met. And I know every member of the Bighorns, both chapters, except one."

"Your bounty."

He nodded. Now that it was in the open, it sounded just as bad as when it played through his head.

"I'm guessing you don't know her real name."

"Before we left for Eagle Crest, I asked a woman in the club if Stormy's her real name or a nickname, and it's real. But I didn't want to know her last name."

"I can see why. You've got some hard thinking to do. Don't discount that your brothers are lawmen and could handle this for you. You don't need to be involved at all."

Wes swallowed hard. "Wouldn't matter. We're related and any bad stuff that goes down will be because of me. I just got the Bighorns to trust me and now..." He trailed off, looking into the distant mountains and wondering how easy it would be to just steal Stormy away and never look back at the club.

"I don't know what I'm doing. I need some time to think on things. I'm hoping you and Winter don't mind if we stay here until I do."

His father gave a shake of his head and roughly pulled him into an embrace. "Always welcome here. You know that. And Winter loves having her boys around. She really likes Stormy too."

"As much as Amaryllis and Cecily?"

Wes didn't know why it mattered so much to him that his family approved of Stormy, but it did.

His father released him and met his stare. "Son, we'll always be happy as long as you are."

He nodded.

"One more thing before we fix this damn gasket."

Wes looked up. "What's that?"

"Don't you think it's about time you start calling Winter your ma? She has been nothing less to you all these years. And I think you both need it."

He nodded, a lump blockading any words he could think to utter.

"Good. Now let's get to work."

* * * * *

As Stormy watched Dirty—or Wes—cross the lawn between barn and house, she couldn't help but think how silly it all was. Her life in the club had never made her ask people's real names. To her, they were Wrench, Breaker, Sundance. None of those were given names and somehow, it had never mattered. They were family.

So when Dirty came along, she hadn't given it much thought. But now that she knew his name was Wes, she wondered what else she didn't know.

Spotting her, he gave that crooked smile that wrapped around her heart and gave it a big hug. But she had things to say and this time she was more nervous than when she'd asked him to bring her to Eagle Crest.

"Sit down?" she asked.

He was grubby and looked tired, but she didn't want to wait and allow life to envelop them before she could get up the gumption to speak what was on her mind.

With a smile, he drew her down to the porch step and held out a hand, clean compared to the rest of him.

"What were you doing?" she asked.

"Fixing a gasket on the tractor. I washed up out back of the barn."

She nodded. Her heart raced.

"What's going on?" he asked quietly. "Did my aunt say something to upset you?"

She hesitated. "Well, she did say something."

"And that was?"

"Your name. Wes."

He went as still as a predator in stalk mode, watching her with a flat stare that almost frightened her. Finally, he broke her gaze and looked down. "I'm sorry I didn't tell you. I should have."

"I'm sorry I never thought to ask. But now I'm curious about what else I don't know about you."

He compressed his lips. "Okay. I'm not sure I want to do this here, after we've had the best two days of my life."

Now she *was* scared. Her stomach fluttered and she had a wave of dizziness. She braced herself. "Tell me what it is."

He searched her gaze. Silhouetted against the beauty of the ranch and distant mountains, she didn't think she'd ever forget how beautiful this man was or how dear to her.

"Stormy, my last name's Roshannon."

She'd heard that somewhere but couldn't place it.

When she didn't respond, he said, "My family, my brothers… they're in the law. Judd's a sheriff and Aiden's a special investigator."

She flashed her gaze to his. "And you?"

"Bounty hunter."

"I'm not sure why you were afraid to tell me."

He made a noise in his throat. "It didn't matter — at first. I came to the club looking for someone who knew my mother, who may be my father. I found Sundance and discovered he's not related to me."

That would be shock enough, but she could see by his face there was more.

"I was just Dirty, hanging out at the club, getting to know the guys — and you. You were the best part, Stormy."

"But…" she prompted.

"But things have changed. I'm looking for a fugitive known to be a Bighorn."

Her blood ran cold. All the secrets between her father and Alexander, his leaving suddenly and staying away so long. She knew he'd been arrested once and was out on bail, but…

Dirty gripped her fingers too tight, and she pulled free.

"I need to ask you something now, Stormy."

She trembled and wrapped her arms around herself. Feeling alone and far from home.

"I need to know if your last name is Bonner."

She didn't have to tell him, was under no obligation. But not answering Dirty made her feel she'd crack in two. He was searching for her brother, that much was apparent. And she was torn, trapped in the middle of what would become a war. Not only between her father, brother and Dirty, but the club would be involved too.

She took a step backward. "It's Bonner."

A breath whooshed from him and he tore off his hat, jamming his fingers through his hair. The action killed her. Knowing he was as ripped apart as she was.

Suddenly, he stood and grabbed her, cradling her face so she couldn't escape as he searched her gaze. "This doesn't change anything between us."

"How can you say that, Dirty? We can't be together."

"Yes, we fucking can. I'm not giving you up. I'm in love with you."

Her world spun on its axis. A woman shouldn't hear a man loves her for the first time when she'd just realized she had to walk away from him.

Oh God, it hurts.

Chapter Ten

"I think you'd better take me back to the club now, Dirty."

Those words had been playing on repeat through his brain for the past twenty-four hours since driving back to the foothills and leaving her at the club.

He'd been riding for hours and still couldn't figure out what the fuck to do. On one hand, his father could be on to something—have one of his brothers or their deputy friends capture Bonner. Then Wes would be in the clear.

His loyalty unquestioned.

But Stormy would still know, and she was the only one who mattered.

When he finally rolled up to the sheriff's office, he hoped to hell Birdie wasn't going to give him crap about seeing Judd, because he wasn't in the mood to be polite.

Luckily, her desk was vacant and Wes walked right into Judd's office.

His brother looked up and went still. "What happened?"

He dropped into the seat across the desk. "My new bounty is Stormy's brother."

He gathered a big breath, chest moving as his lungs expanded, and then blew out it out. "Fuck, that's bad."

"Tell me about it."

"What are you going to do?"

"Hell if I know. It's why I'm here."

Judd nodded and sat back in his seat. "You have a choice not to capture the guy."

"Yes, but she still knows it's my job. I'm not sure she'll forgive me for that."

"Not even if you don't actually take him in? Just ignore that it ever happened?"

Wes stared at his brother. "You know I can't do that. Could you?"

"If it was Cecily, no. Hell, I see your point. Maybe you can find a way to get the guy to turn himself in."

He shook his head. "Unlikely. He's wanted on drug charges and I know it's going on. I've seen some shit."

"Fucking fabulous." Judd's sarcasm told Wes how upset he was by the prospect. "No way of getting him to give himself up."

"Nothing in sight."

"Have someone else haul him in."

"Thought of that. Actually, Dad suggested you or Aiden do it. But Stormy still knows it was me in the long run."

"Anonymous tip wouldn't work either. Damn, you're hemmed into a tight corner, aren't you?"

"Thanks for reminding me."

Judd stared into space for a minute. When he looked back at Wes, he said, "Any chance one of your government friends could do it?"

Wes almost choked on his own tongue. "How the fuck do you know about that?"

"Jesus, if it has to do with a Roshannon, we hear it. Thought you'd know that by now."

"Well, no on that front. I can't ask. I have no contact with anyone these days and I wouldn't want them involved anyway."

In the other room, they heard Birdie humming, back from her break or whatever errand she'd been running.

Judd gnawed his lower lip. "Have you considered taking Stormy out of the club?"

"I'd fucking love to."

"Get the girl, take her to home to the ranch and pop out a couple kids?"

Wes nodded. "And buy her a ring and a pony too. Except I lost her. She's not speaking to me, asked me to take her to the club and drop her off. I don't know what the fuck to do, Judd."

The pain in his own voice made him wince, but Judd's eyes warmed with sympathy. He knew how it was to love a woman.

Judd rocked a bit in his chair. "I can only see one other way, bro."

"What's that?" He hoped to hell it was a sure thing, because he couldn't entertain the possibility of anything less.

"Capture your fugitive and then buy yourself a pair of knee pads."

Confusion pinched his brows together. "For what?"

"Because you'll spend a lot of time on your knees, begging for forgiveness from Stormy."

* * * * *

Stormy counted beer cans as she tossed them in the trash. Eleven, twelve... There had to be more to life for her than this.

She loved the club—she really did. It had been her home forever, the Bighorns her family. But now that she'd experienced Eagle Crest with the man she loved, everything here looked dimmer.

Nothing had changed, but she had. She was ready to find a life of her own, outside the club. She'd been too stupid to believe she'd have it with Dirty.

What they'd had together had been whirlwind, chemistry-packed and bright with promise. And now it was over.

After he'd dropped her at the club, she'd gotten the third degree from DeeDee but had refused to talk

172

about what happened. How could she when it involved her own brother?

He shouldn't have jumped bail and then nobody would be after him. She guessed he'd been arrested for running drugs or dealing them. She didn't condone it, but as you did with people you loved, she analyzed where Alexander had gone wrong.

He wasn't the first person she'd ever seen strung out on something, and being led astray had been the easier path than staying straight.

She sighed and tossed two more cans into the trash. One hit the rim and she had to walk across the room to pick it up. Then she gave the room a glance. It was tidy enough. She was over it.

When she walked into the kitchen, all the ladies looked up at her, concern on their faces. Ignoring them, she went to the refrigerator and grabbed a bottled water.

"You want me to make you a sandwich, sugar?" DeeDee asked, leaning against the counter to eye her better.

Stormy shook her head.

"You can't go on like this, Stormy. Pining over a man is no way to spend your life. You know that. You've seen it before."

She had. Women fell for bikers who would never commit and left the club with broken hearts. But Stormy wasn't only missing Dirty with every cell of her body—the light of her future hopes had been snuffed out. Finally, she'd found what she wanted and now she couldn't have it.

But she was too exhausted to explain to her friends, and besides, it wasn't their business.

Without a word, she left the kitchen and headed for her bedroom. She was about to close the door when DeeDee squeezed into the crack.

"I don't want to talk," Stormy said.

"Well, I don't care. I'm the closest thing to a momma you got, and I'm not watching you suffer anymore."

"Fine." Stormy stepped back to allow the woman inside. DeeDee closed the door and leaned against it.

"Remember when you were younger, you'd have bad dreams? I'd make you talk it out and then you'd feel better. Sometimes just saying it aloud makes it go away."

She shook her head. "This isn't going away."

DeeDee grabbed her hand and pulled her to sit on the bed. "Men can be asses. Did he do something to hurt you?"

How to answer that? Not really—Dirty, or Wes, was just doing his job. He was supposed to capture Alexander. It wasn't his fault her brother was dumb and had gotten himself in that trouble.

DeeDee squeezed her hand. "Tell me what's going on. If that man hurt you in some way, I'll send Sam and the boys out to teach him a lesson."

Stormy grunted, almost with amusement. That was the Bighorn way — protecting their own even if it meant doing wrong to fix a wrong. Plus, she'd like to see those guys take on someone of Dirty's size.

"Girl, you always were stubborn to a fault. Like a kid who won't eat her vegetables. Just tell me what's going on."

Stormy felt terrible for causing her friend distress. Pulling her hand free, she gripped her fingers together in her lap and stared at them. Thinking of Dirty's callused fingers, the way they felt so good against her smoother skin.

"He isn't who I thought he was."

DeeDee's eyes were sympathetic. "It's hard to know a person in the short time you were together."

"That's not what I mean. He's a lawman. A bounty hunter."

Something skittered over DeeDee's face, and Stormy wouldn't be surprised one bit if her friend knew everything about Alexander's problems. Things Stormy was kept in the dark about, protected as usual by her father.

"He just got a new fugitive to hunt... and it's Alexander."

DeeDee nodded, unsurprised as Stormy had guessed. And yet paler at the news.

"So once he found out you're his sister, Dirty dumped you?"

Stormy shook her head. "No, I dumped him. Asked him to bring me home."

"Well, we aren't exactly going to accept him as a Bighorn after he captures one of our own."

It was a miracle they'd accepted Dirty at all, but he'd proved himself. The tests her father had put him through had been all bullshit and for show — day after day Dirty was here working alongside the guys, supporting the club's causes and doing his best for them had been the real tests.

"Stormy, did you ask Dirty to back off, forget about that particular bounty?"

She shook her head. "I hardly spoke to him after he told me the truth. But asking him wouldn't have helped. *I* know what should have rightfully been done, and that is for him to do his job and make my brother show up for court."

DeeDee remained silent.

"I can't ask a man like Dirty to compromise himself, mess with the way he earns his living. If he did, how could we go on together? The problem would never go away and resentment would build." She shook her head. "No, what we had was too beautiful to allow that to happen."

Stormy's voice trailed off, full of tears. Her face crumpled.

"Oh, sweetie." DeeDee hugged her tight and rocked her lightly for long minutes as Stormy spent all the emotion she thought she'd gotten out in the days since last seeing Dirty.

She sniffled, and DeeDee went out of the room for a minute, coming back with a box of tissue. Stormy took several and blew her nose and mopped at her eyes.

"Better?" DeeDee asked, taking a seat on the bed again.

She shrugged. "Nothing's changed. Nothing can."

"The pain of love lost takes a while to heal, but it will."

"I don't think so. I want him and nobody else. And it isn't only him I love. I love his ranch, his way of life, of looking at things. It's the best mix of his world and mine—here." She waved at her small, tidy room.

"I was afraid of that." DeeDee caught her gaze.

"You don't think I should ever leave the club."

"I didn't say that. There are plenty of Bighorns who don't live here and immerse themselves in this life as deeply as we do. Think of Sundance's wife. When she's here, she loves her man and fits in like the best of them. But then she knows when it's time to head back to her own life."

She nodded in understanding. "Dirty came and went like that. And each time he'd return, I'd love him a little bit more until he consumed my world so much that I wanted to go and be part of his as well."

DeeDee stroked the hair from her cheekbone. "There's nothing wrong with that kind of living. Any life you choose is the right one for you."

Stormy looked up into her friend's eyes. "I don't know what to do."

"I wish I could offer advice, but I don't know either. I can only say let time and distance make the decisions for now."

Mulling that over, Stormy nodded. "Thank you, DeeDee. You're always here for me. But you're wrong about something."

DeeDee's eyes widened as if she'd let her down. "What's that?"

"You're not like my momma because you're not nearly old enough. But I do think of you as a wonderful big sister."

"Ohhh, come here." She wrapped her up in a hug.

When they broke apart, the guys were back, the front of the club noisy as ever. But this time, their voices projecting through the walls weren't laughing or amused.

"They sound serious," she said.

"Too serious." DeeDee got up and walked out with Stormy behind her.

In the main room, the guys were all on their feet, shoulders tense as they spoke in quieter tones.

Stormy spotted her father and hurried up to him, putting a hand on his arm. "What's going on?"

When he looked at her, she saw creases around his eyes he didn't often wear. "There was a big shootout next county over. An officer shot four times."

The next county over could be north, south, east or west, but her heart stopped at the word officer. Crimes like that weren't taken lightly in any part of the country, but in these smaller towns of Wyoming, they were unheard of.

Shock rippled through her.

"Who was the officer? Do you know?" It hit her hard that it could be one of Wes's brothers, who were both in the law.

Her dad shook his head. "No word released yet. We just heard—there's talk all over the place. People are banding together to help the guy's family."

"What can I do? I'll write up an event."

Sundance heard what she said and turned to her. "Make something up. I trust you. We'd like to raise as much money as we can right now while the man's got a life to fight for."

This was the part of the Bighorns she loved. For all their shortcomings, they were there in the community in a way many people or even other organizations weren't.

She stood and listened to the talk for another moment before hurrying off to the office to slap together a fundraiser. Right now, the world had bigger problems, making her own look small in comparison, and she was glad for the perspective.

* * * * *

Wes's back muscles strained with each wrench of the rope in his grip. But the calf wasn't cooperating and the heifer'd stopped pushing. "C'mon, momma. A little help would be nice."

"I'm in agreement," his dad said, adjusting his hold on the second handle of the calf puller. The pair of them had been working for long minutes, soaked in sweat and muck from the birthing.

But getting a live calf on the ground was the most important thing. Wes would pull all day if it meant saving a life.

"She's bearing down. Pull," his father ordered.

They put their combined strength into it and the forelegs slid out of the cow.

"More," Wes urged.

"Oh my God, Matthias."

They looked around at Winter's voice. She was flushed red as if she'd run the whole way from the house.

"What is it?" He stopped pulling as hard but retained his grip and the pressure on the calf.

She ran into the barn and stopped. "Officer was shot. No one can find Judd."

Wes and Matthias let go at the same time. Wes's heart lurched against his chest wall so painfully that he grunted.

"What do you mean can't find him? Who can't?"

"Birdie hasn't heard from him. Cecily either."

The two women who had Judd by the balls were his secretary and wife. Wes's bowels cramped.

"I'll call him." Heedless of the slime on his hands, he grabbed his phone from his back pocket and dialed Judd. While he pressed the phone to his ear, his parents embraced, clinging to each other, each white with what this could mean for them, their family, their universe.

"He's not answering." Wes ended the call and stared at them. "Have they disclosed the patient's name yet? Has Cecily gotten a call?"

His mother shook her head.

"Aiden," his dad said.

Wes was dialing Aiden before the final syllable crossed his father's lips. The cow gave a long, low moo of distress. They couldn't stop the birthing process, but they couldn't ignore what might have happened to one of their own either.

"Fuck, Wes," Aiden's voice filled his ear. "Have you heard?"

"Just now. Who is it? Is it Judd?"

"No one will tell me. Goddammit, this can't be good."

"Use that twin link of yours. Can't you feel him or something?"

"Doesn't work that way, brother. I wish to fuck it did. Fucking hell." Aiden's voice was strained in a way that told Wes that Judd's twin was losing it.

"Okay, calm down. We have to find someone who knows something. Birdie and Cecily don't know where Judd's at."

"I know. I called them first. Shit!"

"Where are you? Anywhere near the hospital that way?"

"Hell no. I'm halfway across the goddamn state trying to find some asshole who stole a ten-thousand-dollar bull. I'm on my way, driving as fast as I can."

"Don't get into an accident. I'm going to make another call. I'll be in touch, Aiden."

When he got Cecily on the line, she was crying. She didn't bother with the formality of saying hello but just said, "Oh my God, Wes. I can't find Judd and someone's been shot."

"It's okay, honey. Just stay calm. Judd's known to go off on his own on a case without giving word every time."

"Birdie always knows where he is."

"Well, not this time."

Their mother threw Wes a wild-eyed look. The cow was bearing down but the calf's legs just moved in and out without going anywhere.

"Cecily, where are you?"

"At home. I don't know what to do."

"Sit tight. You're not in any shape to drive. I'm going to dig a bit and then I'll call you back."

He stuffed his phone in his pocket, grabbed the rope around the calf and pulled with every ounce of his strength. Adrenaline, fear and desperation were on his side, and the calf came out in two pulls. It slid onto the hay.

His dad released his mom long enough to dump a bucket of water over its face to get it breathing. It lay there staring as the momma cow twisted around and began licking it.

Wes hurriedly untied the rope from the calf's legs. His phone was in his hand the minute the rope was free. He walked out of the barn and started rapid-dialing everyone he knew.

First the hospital, who would only disclose that the officer was in surgery and his name couldn't be released.

He called Judd's deputies and even the district attorney who was close friends with Judd and often shot skeet with him. He was just ringing off with the man when a call came in.

When he heard the familiar tone of his brother in his ear, Wes's knees went weak. "Judd, where the fuck have you been?"

"That dipshit Erikson had me running halfway across the county trying to arrest his stupid ass."

"Everyone thinks you've been shot. Including your wife."

"I got her messages. Called her first. I'm on my way home right now to her. She's really upset."

"No fucking shit."

"Glad to hear everyone cares about me so much. Aiden said he's going to wring my neck when he sees me."

"Good, then he'll take care of it before I do." Wes felt a grin spread over his face, relieved that his brother was safe and whole.

But a heavy weight for the officer who'd been shot filled his chest.

"Judd, do you know who it is?"

"Yeah. It's Mason."

"The marshal?"

"Yeah, he was here to deliver a subpoena and was shot point blank."

"Jesus Christ."

"Yeah, he's in bad shape. Cecily's on the line again. I gotta go, bro. She's in a delicate condition and I don't want her getting too upset. Tell Mom and Dad I'm okay and I'll call soon."

Wes rang off and stepped into the barn. "That was Judd. He's all right."

His momma's legs went out from under her and she sat down hard in the hay, legs sprawled out like the newborn calf's. Wes and his father knelt with her and shared an embrace and a prayer of thanksgiving.

Wes's mind spun around the events that had just taken place. The calf and mother were fine and so was his brother. Judd had scared the hell out of all of them, and Wes wouldn't let him live that down for a long time, though he figured Cecily would do most of the honors.

When Wes had spoken with her, the terror in her voice had reached deep down inside Wes and hooked his guts. Judd was her life, her heart and soul. Thank God he was okay for her.

But it left Wes wondering. If he'd been in trouble, who would worry about him that way?

* * * * *

The bikers were all over the county collecting donations at various bike shops, convenience stores and VFW halls. The flyers Stormy had made were taken by the piles and handed out everywhere a Bighorn could ride.

That night when the word came in that the officer had made it through surgery and was in a guarded stable condition, the Bighorns were ready to party.

Stormy was as happy to hear as anyone and so relieved to know it wasn't a Roshannon man who'd been injured. But she wasn't in the mood to join in the celebration.

She moved toward her bedroom when a big hand wrapped around her shoulder. She glanced back to see her dad, looking somber.

"Can I talk to you?"

"I guess." She led him to her room, which seemed to be the new place to have deep discussions.

He faced her. "I know all about Dirty."

She blinked.

"DeeDee told Sam, who told me."

"Shit. I should have known she wouldn't keep it to herself."

"It's good she didn't."

Stormy sighed. "At least you know he's after Alexander and you can give him a head's up."

He stared at her for such a long time that Stormy's heart began to pound.

"What's going on, Dad?"

"I talked your brother into turning himself in."

She jerked. "What?" Her voice came out as a rasp.

Her father reached for her, holding her by the shoulders, almost holding her up. She felt like she'd collapse at the news and couldn't begin to process what it all meant.

"Your brother has some problems he needs to face. And knowing how much it was affecting you—hurting you—made me realize I needed to talk to him about going to the cops and handing himself over."

"Oh my God."

Her father tugged her against his chest roughly and held her head to him. "I love you, Stormy. I'll never have another daughter and I don't want to lose you. Each day I see you getting sadder and pulling away from us more. Well, I know you love that man, and I don't even care what he does for a living. He's a good man who can do right by you, that much is clear to me."

She pushed back to stare at her father's face. "Are you serious?"

"You know I'm no good at making things up. Remember those bedtime stories about the crippled reindeer?"

A laugh burst from her, half sob. "So... Alexander's turned himself in?"

He nodded. "He was sick of running, sick of looking over his shoulder all the time. And ready to clean up his act."

She swallowed hard. "I'm proud of him."

"Me too." He looked into her eyes. "And I'm proud of the woman you are. Giving up the man you love for your family... Well, it was loyal to a fault. But now you're free to go your own way, baby girl."

A tear trickled from the corner of her eye.

"Go find your man and make a life together."

She threw her arms around him and he plucked her off her feet. "I can't believe I have your blessing."

"Blessing? Hell, I did the hard work for you."

"What do you mean?"

187

He set her down again and grinned. "Dirty's in the other room waiting."

Her jaw dropped and for a moment, she didn't think she could move a muscle. But then her brain caught up and she shot out the door. Searching the bodies filling the front room for one big, muscled man.

When she spotted him, her heart tumbled. She tripped forward, and he strode up to her. Picking her up and slamming his mouth over hers in one move. His scents flooded in—leather, man, grass. A complete mixture of everything she loved in life and held dear.

He pulled back to stare at her. A growl left him as he moved back in for a kiss. Plunging his tongue into her mouth. Cheers erupted around them, and she knew that everything was going to be okay. Her worlds were melding together and Wes's arms were around her again.

Epilogue

The warm fingers of the Wyoming breeze trailed through Stormy's hair. Judd's and Aiden's wives would kill her if the curls they'd spent hours putting into her hair fell out before she got a chance to walk down the aisle.

This was really happening. Eagle Crest had been set up with a hundred chairs tied with pretty white satin bows and the white tent was erected for dinner and dancing. She was powdered, primped and zipped into her gown with the simple lace beading.

And her cowgirl boots were perfectly broken in for this day. As soon as her sister-in-law-to-be, Amaryllis, had heard she was marrying Wes on the family ranch, she'd insisted she needed something blue and took Stormy shopping for just the right pair.

Stormy peered around the corner of the house where she'd walk out to meet her groom, and Cecily slapped her arm.

"He can't see you or you'll have bad luck!" She rubbed at her small baby bump growing under her bridesmaid gown.

Stormy didn't know if she should giggle or burst into tears. Her emotions were all over the place.

Since Wes had brought her back to Eagle Crest, she'd felt a sense of new beginnings. They'd spent the past months together, working, living and loving. When he'd dropped to one knee and presented her with a ring, all her dreams had manifested into one happy future.

She held her eyes wide to keep from crying or smudging her mascara. When the man rounded the corner, she widened them even more.

"Dad! You look amazing in a tux."

"And you couldn't look more beautiful, though I'd like to see some black biker boots instead of the blue." He gave her a crooked grin. In a tux that fit him like a perfectly tailored second skin, he looked far from the biker who'd raised her.

She peeked around the corner again. "I see a lot of bikes." Excitement sounded in her voice. She couldn't wait to celebrate with her Bighorn family.

"Yeah, they're all out there waiting for your big entrance. Speaking of..." He offered his arm just as the music began.

Stormy wrapped her arm around his waist and squeezed him before taking his arm. "I'm glad to have you with me today."

"Happy to do it." They took their place. Ahead of them, Amaryllis and Cecily made their way one by one down the aisle to where all the Roshannon men stood. But Stormy's eyes skipped right over Judd and Aiden to gape at the man she was marrying.

The Wyoming sun seemed to beam down only on him, making his thick dark hair gleam and accentuate the chiseled lines of his face. The white of his shirt glowed against his tan neck.

Her heart skipped a beat and for a second, she didn't know what to do.

Wes's gaze pinned her where she stood.

Her father looked down at her. "He's waiting for you."

They took the first step onto the white satin pathway running through the emerald grass and straight to the makeshift altar where her man stood.

She didn't realize the walk had ended until Wes's hands enveloped hers. She tilted her head back to meet his gaze.

Warm, steely gray and burning with love and a trace of tears.

She wanted to go on tiptoe and kiss him already, but there were words to say. Her biker family and her new family, the Roshannons, were here to witness her vowing her love for Wes for the rest of her days.

"You may kiss the bride."

Shocked at how fast the ceremony had drawn to an end, she turned and tossed the bouquet at the ladies who'd come with Bighorns and threw her arms around her husband's neck.

* * * * *

191

Wes couldn't take his eyes off his new bride. All that white beading clung to her curves like a Harley on the highway. He couldn't wait to take either for a ride.

She stood laughing with some of the ladies from the club, throwing Wes covert glances that made him look around for a place to hide away with her. Being surrounded by family and friends had him grinding his teeth and waiting for the opportunity to arise.

A beer appeared before his face, and he took it from his brother. Aiden followed Wes's gaze to Stormy.

"Who knew you'd do so well for yourself?" Aiden brought the beer to his lips.

Judd jumped into the group. "Who did well? Oh yeah, I never expected Wes to marry anything but a horse."

Wes gave a wry smile and took a swig of the beer. "We had a rough start, for sure." Looking at Stormy's beautiful face in profile, he couldn't believe how far they'd come. Through the proverbial hell and high water. In his opinion, thrust together by fate. His search for family had taken him to the Bighorns and he'd walked away with so much more than he imagined possible.

"So what's next for Mr. and Mrs. Wes Roshannon?" Judd asked.

"I've been thinking of staying right here, helping Dad and building a house on the land, that is if nobody cares."

Both brothers shrugged. "Why would we care? The land is yours as much as ours, even if you weren't actually our blood brother."

He clinked beers with each before spying his opportunity to steal his bride away. "Excuse me." He shoved his beer at Judd.

Chuckles sounded behind him as he made a beeline for Stormy. He caught her elbow and pulled her away from the Bighorns with a smile. He placed his lips to Stormy's ear and whispered, "I need you. Alone."

Her face flushed pink and the ladies giggled, waving her away.

Wes led his wife by the hand around the side of the barn. The party hadn't reached back here, and he was grateful.

"Wes, where are we going?"

He glanced back at her. "I need a moment alone with this beautiful woman wearing my ring." He skimmed his thumb over the band he'd just slipped onto her finger.

He drew her to a spot of cool shade. He'd long ago shucked his tuxedo jacket and the bowtie. His shirt was open at the collar and the sleeves rolled but he was still too hot.

What he was about to do would have them both drenched in sweat and sticking together in seconds.

"Oh no. I don't know if I like that grin," she said.

"You will." He grabbed her ass and hitched her against him. A rough sigh left her, and he realized how pent-up she was too.

"Mmm. I fucking want you, Mrs. Roshannon."

A shiver ran through her, and he couldn't resist claiming her full, plump lips. As their mouths melded together, she reached down between his legs, settling her warm hand over his bulge.

He groaned, and she answered with a hitching breath as he located her hardened nipple beneath the beading of her dress. He squeezed it nice and slow, pulling a cry from her.

He drew back, and they stared at each other for a heartbeat before she went for his pants and he shimmied her dress up over her hips. In seconds, he had his fingers buried in her soaking heat and she fisted his cock, angling it where they both wanted it — needed it.

"Oh my God, Wes. Take me. Now."

He joined them with one jerk of his hips. She gave a muffled cry, which he swallowed with his deep kiss. Tongues swirling, passion flaring. Their own wedding celebration sounding low in the background and birds chirping as he consummated their vows.

"I'm glad you took me away. I couldn't wait for this." She bit into his lower lip, raising a growl from him.

He pushed his cock deeper with each stroke. Her inner muscles tensed around him, and he knew she wasn't going to last long. He wanted her screaming his name, but they probably should keep it quiet or risk embarrassing his mother to death.

He sucked on the soft skin behind her ear, and she grabbed onto his shoulders harder, grinding against him. The rustle of their clothing music on the wind.

"Dirty..."

"Mmm. I love when you call me that."

She looked into his eyes as a squeaking gasp left her. He slammed into her pussy one more stroke and watched her shatter. Eyes fluttering closed on her release. He couldn't hold back anymore. He cupped her ass and dragged her against him for two more strokes before he launched over the ledge too.

Her pussy squeezed him hard as he shot into her. Their combined moans ending on heavy breathing.

He cradled her lovely face in his hands and stared into her eyes.

"Think anyone will know?" She giggled.

"My brothers will. I'm pretty sure they each sneaked away with their wives on their wedding days too."

"So it's family tradition."

"Guess so." He chuckled and slowly detached himself from her body, letting her thong slide back into place and her gown float down around her little blue cowgirl boots.

She pressed her hands against his chest as if trying to regain equilibrium. He repositioned his clothing and was presentable again.

"I have another reason for believing you live up to your nickname of Dirty."

He chuckled.

"I'll never forget that as long as I live."

"I hope not. I won't either. I promise not to forget a single minute I spend with you, baby." He drew her to him and brushed his lips over hers again, lightly this time. "I love you."

"Forever." She smiled the way a woman smiles when she has the world of happiness stretched before her and no shadows in sight.

READ ON FOR A SNEAK PEEK OF SOMETHING ABOUT A MOUNTAIN MAN

If the mountain didn't claim a man by way of a blizzard or bears, starvation would do the trick. Ryan was damn hungry — all the time. Hunting, fishing and trapping was a constant need up here in the Wyoming mountains, when he wasn't tending his small homestead in the Big Horns, that was.

Amidst his animals he had a solid horse to get out of the mountains, not that he ever wanted to. A pair of goats for milk, a handful of chickens and twelve pigs. Soon to be more, since a sow was brooding. If he didn't get a shed built for her right quick, and some heat pumped into it, the piglets would end up being claimed by the mountain too. Freezing nighttime temperatures weren't kind to young.

Torn between leaving the small plot of land he called his own to hunt and satisfy his gnawing hunger and staying right here and getting a start on the shed was making Ryan grouchy.

Well, grouchier than usual.

He dropped onto a makeshift stool he'd created with his own two hands — maimed as they were with the two missing fingers on his right. He picked up a branch and started shaving curls of wood onto the cold ashes of the fire.

Fire was just as essential as a good pair of boots and a rifle in these parts. Besides providing warmth and cooking his food, it kept predators away from his homestead.

The knife rasping on the branch was the only sound he heard besides birds and squirrels playing in the underbrush. The whisper of the mountain air was a constant music, and it sure beat the noise of gunfire.

He shifted on the stool, and the joints strained under his weight. Then he heard it.

A whine, soft but clear. He went dead still like he'd been spotted by an enemy sniper, straining to hear it again.

There. He dropped the branch and snapped his knife shut, on his feet and moving toward the noise, grabbing his gun on the way. If it was another bear in his animal pen, he'd be eating good without leaving the homestead.

As he neared the chicken coop, he stopped walking and extended his senses. Hearing the heartbeat of the mountain and underneath that, the same whine.

A chicken squawked and something darted away from the fence, rolling as if it'd been shot. But Ryan hadn't even raised his rifle.

The brown and white critter didn't make it two steps before Ryan lunged, clamping it firmly by the scruff. Thinking it an odd-colored coon, he held it up.

"A puppy." His voice cracked with disuse. What was a friggin' puppy doing on the mountain—his mountain? There wasn't anybody on the east face besides him. Nobody was stupid enough to hike up this way either, not with the spring weather still so sporadic.

The pup squirmed in his hold and he drew it closer to his chest to examine it. Couldn't be a wild dog either—he'd never seen any up here. It was possibly a coyote pup, though it looked nothing like those animals.

"How'd you get here?"

The animal's stubby tail wiggled to and fro so fast the whole body vibrated with it. Ryan shook his head. A damn dog. He couldn't eat a dog.

He set it on the ground. Now that it was on all fours, he saw it was lankier than he'd originally thought when it was scrambling in fright away from the chickens. Perhaps four or five months old, with longer legs that promised it would get much bigger if fed up right.

That was the trouble—it looked hungrier than him.

He watched it for a minute as it sniffed the perimeter of the fence protecting the chickens. The rooster, used to scaring off predators and protecting his harem, ran at the pup flapping his wings.

Another whine and the puppy shied away.

"Damn." Ryan's voice wasn't even getting warmed up. After all, he'd only spoken a few words in a month or so, and he liked it that way.

The pup turned from the coop and rushed Ryan's boots, pouncing at the lace. He caught the loop in his sharp puppy teeth and tugged.

"Get off, you little shit." The words came out as a grumble, but he heard something in his own tone that startled him.

Amusement.

When was the last time he'd laughed?

The answer was easy—back with his platoon. Jennings had cracked a joke about one of the corporals that had made Ryan chuckle. Then that same hour, they'd been geared up and rolling toward the village that was under heavy fire. And that fucking photojournalist was in the thick of it.

Livvy.

He slammed the door on the mental image her name conjured and stared down at the nuisance at his feet.

"C'mon, dumbass. Let's find you something to eat before you cut through my bootlace." He took off toward the cabin, a one-room structure of rough-hewn wood. The door was sturdy enough to keep predators out and what little he kept inside safe.

The pup stood at the open door, looking up at him.

"Suit yourself," he said, not sure if he liked hearing his vocal cords beginning to smooth out with the practice of speaking.

He turned for the small kitchen area he'd rigged with a basin for use as a sink and a single cupboard nailed to the wall above. It hung a little crooked, but he'd only noticed after the fact and hadn't bothered adjusting it.

The sole window in the place, a skylight in the center of the ceiling, cast light on the cupboard. Inside was a cloth sack containing the only food he had left in the world—three thin chunks of meat dried to a tooth-breaking toughness. Emergency rations.

Somehow feeding the pup wasn't what he'd consider an emergency, but he couldn't let an animal starve, now could he? He was considered a stern asshole among his fellow Marines and a moody fucker by those he'd encountered after getting blown up in Afghanistan.

But he was still human enough to have a heart, even if it was gray and shriveled.

He grabbed two pieces of jerky and walked to the door. He tossed one at the puppy, and he scampered to get it, clamping it in his jaws and shaking it.

Ryan snorted. "You don't gotta kill it. It's already dead, believe me." The meat was tougher than puppy teeth could probably manage, too. God knew Ryan'd about broken his jaw on the last piece.

The puppy plopped into the dirt, and bracing the meat between its paws, began to work the sinew until he was able to soften it enough to swallow.

Ryan watched him for a while before tossing him the second piece. The pup's face was spotted white and brown and reminded him of a dog he'd had as a kid called Freckles. What was he supposed to do with a dog? He couldn't turn it out onto the mountain—it would die. Even if it was able to catch a squirrel or a rabbit, hunting was hard in these parts.

He could take the animal down the mountain into the nearest town. Someone would take it in—people were always on the lookout for good dogs. But that meant taking days away from his own livestock and besides, he had traps to check.

Not to mention he had no desire to step foot in town anytime soon, though if he wanted to put in that garden that would make his winters easier, he'd need seeds. The post office didn't send men up the mountain to deliver mail to recluses.

The only person he'd seen in nearly a year was his old military buddy Aiden Roshannon. The man refused to let Ryan go without a visit every few months, but luckily Aiden didn't make him talk about his time in the military. Neither of them had a desire to discuss that.

That was the second time his mind had touched on the military and the sun hadn't completely cracked over the ridge yet. Days like this were never fun.

He closed the cabin door and returned to making his fire. In seconds he had orange flames leaping. He breathed in the scent of wood smoke and sighed at the calm it gave him. The scent meant he was alone. He was okay. Far from anybody he could harm.

Livvy.

He shook her off.

Sitting on the stool was making his thigh cramp, and he couldn't afford for the old injury to flare up, not when he had to walk the trap line today. He stood and stretched. The pup jumped at his boot again and released a growling bark that wouldn't scare a flea off his own skinny back.

"If you're sticking around, you'd better learn to leave my bootlace alone." He considered the pup. Just when did he decide the animal was sticking around?

Ryan got a pot of water boiling and used it to wash, stripping down to the skin and splashing the water over his back and then scrubbing his face and the nastier parts. About once a week he bathed in the creek, but he didn't have anyone to impress and he'd been far dirtier in some of his Afghanistan days.

What had that sweet little photojournalist called the war? *The war that never ended and no longer had a mission.* That about summed it up.

Dammit, that was the third time she'd popped into his mind. Stupid of him, when she sure as hell wasn't sitting around thinking about him. But Livvy ranked up there with his momma, rest her soul, how much his leg ached and his growling belly as things that he could never stop thinking about.

At least he'd stopped caring about his missing fingers. The pinky and ring fingers weren't as necessary as he'd once thought—he could still pull a trigger fine.

Yeah, the mountain was the best place for him. But now he had the added dilemma of feeding a dog with no name.

He didn't like to butcher his livestock at this time of year when wildlife was so plentiful. He'd save the livestock for later in the season after they were fattened by foraging on the sweet grasses growing at the base of the east face of the mountain. The chickens were in some funk, though, and hadn't been laying eggs consistently.

"First thing's first. I get a real breakfast because no way am I gnawing on that last piece of jerky." After standing around naked, the cool mountain air had dried his skin. He dressed and strode to the coop. The pup trotted at his heels. He tossed a look over his shoulder.

Yeah, the dog looked a lot like the one he had as a boy.

"Well, Freckles, if my hens are lucky, they left me a couple eggs to fry. Otherwise, we'll have fire-roasted chicken wings for breakfast."

* * * * *

Damn, it felt good to be out with her camera again. The past weeks cooped up in the hospital had just about driven her crazy. She'd begged her boss, who'd come to visit her, to bring her camera, but he'd refused, telling her that she needed to recuperate so she could take the next big assignment. An Alaskan adventure following a fishing fleet. Dangerous stuff, but no more dangerous than her year spent in Afghanistan.

She adjusted a setting on her equipment and took a still shot of the tree line that abruptly cut off on the mountain slope, the last bit of vegetation before the conditions were too high and harsh to support life.

And this was where Ryan Stone had been hiding all these months.

She prided herself on her outdoors skills and could navigate almost anywhere in the world with nothing more than some latitude and longitude coordinates and a compass. So finding one ornery Marine who didn't want to be found was right in her wheelhouse.

Although she had to admit he'd done a hell of a job camouflaging himself this time. It had taken at least twenty phone calls to his old buddies and platoon sergeants to try to locate him. Finally, she'd gotten a tip from someone to call a Wyoming lawman by the name of Roshannon.

He'd been hesitant to give her the intel, but if her navigation skills were good, her persuasion skills were excellent. Plus, it helped that Roshannon had a toddler and wanted some family photos taken.

She let her camera rest against her chest as she got her bearings of east from northeast and set off toward the spot Roshannon had told her Stone was living. There was one narrow path that seemed to be used for horses, and she stuck to it. But in spots where it had washed away, she had to use her instincts and some guesswork.

The pines were thicker around the east side of the ridge, and she had to pick her way slowly. She took her time, trying not to twist an ankle or something worse. And she snapped photos.

Of a mountain bluebird and another gray one that she couldn't put name to. They flitted from branch to branch, seeming to follow her, chattering all the way. A fog had rolled in this morning and had delayed her coming up the mountain the minute she woke up. The thick white patches still clung to the tree line and added ambience to her photos.

She wanted to capture the very air — how it smelled, felt in her lungs.

Livvy snapped more photos and tried to keep her mind off meeting Stone. What was she going to say to him? She'd thought about that a lot since making the decision to come here. But she always came up blank.

What was there to say? Hey, Stone, thanks for saving my life back there, good to see you, have a great life?

She'd talked and joked with all the Marines, but she'd considered Stone a friend. Even though he was a man of few words, she'd always felt him near her, watching out for her.

Though he hadn't held back his opinions on her being there in the first place. He'd flat out told her she had no business being in that dangerous situation, and in the end, he'd been right.

A crack of a twig had her turning her head slowly. She'd been warned of bears and carried a canister of bear spray as well as a Ruger, one on each hip like a gunslinger.

A dusty brown coat came into view through the deep evergreen of the pines and Livvy moved her camera slowly into position to get a photo of the deer. Head upraised in alert, ears forward, listening.

She didn't realize a smile had taken over her face until the deer moved away. Livvy continued on, taking everything in.

She had to admit, it was a beautiful place to live. So different from what they'd known in Afghanistan with the endless sand, beiges and browns. Here, it was just budding with spring, though it was late in the year compared to lower regions. The snow was off the mountainside, and the rush of water could be heard in any direction she turned.

How must Stone feel to live here on his own? She had to wonder at his state of mind.

Her stomach knotted. Her biggest fear was finding him beyond reach—out of his mind with post-traumatic stress disorder and too distant for her to make real contact with him.

Realistically, she knew their relationship hadn't been all that close. Sure, there had been an almost-kiss, but nothing had happened in the end.

He'd drawn away before she could press her lips to those hard, unsmiling ones of his that she'd been wanting to taste for a long time.

Then the next day, after the explosion, he'd been gone and she was off to the nearest military hospital to have the shrapnel removed from her neck, followed by what seemed like hundreds of stitches.

When she'd spoken to Roshannon, she'd gotten the nerve to ask if Stone had lost his leg as had been rumored. A beat of silence had made her heart beat wildly, but he'd said no.

Well, she just had to find the man and see for herself how rough a shape he was in.

She made the rest of the hike faster without stopping to take pictures. As she peered through the pines into a small clearing, the faint cluck of chickens reached her.

She stepped out and looked around at what Stone had built for himself. A few small buildings and some fencing. A camp yard with a stool and a fire that was still burning low.

Oh my God. He's here.

Roshannon had warned her that he went out pretty often to hunt and check traps. She was glad she wouldn't have to wait for him. After all, a combat veteran coming in from hunting to find a stranger sitting at his campfire wouldn't feel all that friendly. And she didn't know Stone's current state of mind.

She let out the breath she'd been holding and walked around the side of a building. An animal grunted, and she saw the big black body of a pig. Then more. It seemed the biggest building wasn't Stone's cabin but a pig barn.

The animals started grunting like crazy when they saw her, probably thinking it was feeding time. Without thought, she raised her camera and had a few closeups of dirt-flecked snouts and piggy eyes eagerly looking for food.

A bleat had her searching for the source only to discover a goat standing on top of what looked like a doghouse with a sloping roof. Inside, another goat peered out of the hay bed it lay on.

So, Stone was a real homesteader. Somehow it pleased her knowing he wasn't up here alone. The animals weren't great company, but they were something to care for. A man who was deep in the throes of depression wouldn't be able to keep his animals so well-cared for, right?

She pressed her long braid over her shoulder and circled the animal pens to find the chicken coop. A rooster strutted along the fence.

Getting into a crouch, Livvy snapped a few pics and then stood and turned her camera on the cabin itself.

Man, it was rough, but she could envision Stone here. The place was built like a tank with a door that would guard a fortress, crisscrossed with thick planks of wood. Was he trying to keep things out or himself in?

She got her lens into focus and got a few different angles on shots, including a great one with a bit of the dirt ground leading up to the house bearing one big size-twelve boot print.

"What the fuck are you doing here?" The voice was unlike anything she'd heard, and she shot to her feet, whirling in the same movement.

Holy shit.

The man standing before her wasn't Stone. At least not the Stone she knew. This guy was just as big and broad, with biceps like big guns on top of a tank. But his appearance was shocking.

She couldn't get past the tangled, long brown hair or the thick nest of his beard hanging in the center of his chest to look for his past injuries.

"Stone?"

"What the fuck are you doing here?" Asking the second time around still wasn't unlocking her mind or her tongue. Was she really looking at the man she'd known a year ago?

His eyes weren't even the same. Darker than the old hazel she remembered. With a hard glint like steel or granite that could have been mined from this very mountain.

And they felt cold.

She gaped at him. Her hands moved on their own, and she raised her camera.

He made a slicing motion as if to bat it out of her grasp. "If you come near me with that thing, I'll smash it."

Dear God, his voice. Had it been wrecked by the hit they'd both taken? She'd suffered the injury to her neck, but he must have had more extensive injuries than she'd learned of.

His gaze flashed to her neck and the scarf tied around it and then traveled over her body right to her sturdy walking boots.

She stood rooted under his stare, unable to move or breathe. But she could direct her eyes and did so, roaming down to his boots and back up. Jeans, the thighs dirty from him wiping his hands there. A smear of blood across the denim that pulled so perfectly across those thick muscles.

Her chest burned from lack of oxygen and she drew a shaky breath.

As she let her gaze trace back over his muscled chest in a plaid cotton shirt to that beard and finally his face... She had no words.

This was a mountain man, and far from what she'd envisioned she'd find in Stone. He looked like a wild thing just emerged from a cave ready to snap her head off.

Well, he'd already threatened to smash her precious camera. Though she did carry a spare in the pack on her back, along with a few changes of clothes she hoped would get her through a short stay here with Stone while she figured out how to thank him for what he'd done for her.

She opened her mouth. Closed it.

"Woman, you never did have sense. You traveled here on your own?" He glanced around and then his gaze crash-landed on her again. A heavy warmth moved through her as she recognized that look he wore. Yeah, this was Stone. The man who'd held back from kissing her and walked away looking so damn tormented she'd wanted to beg for him to come back.

His eyes lost some of that cold glare and burned with something she remembered.

"My God, Stone."

He jerked at her tone. His fingers convulsed at his sides, and she realized one hand looked oddly-shaped. Like a pincer.

She couldn't have prepared herself for this and any words she might have rehearsed couldn't be said now.

"Here I thought I was the one who'd forgotten how to talk. What do you have to say for yourself, woman?"

GRAB YOUR COPY OF SOMETHING ABOUT A MOUNTAIN MAN

Em Petrova

Em Petrova is a USA Today Bestselling Author who was raised by hippies in the wilds of Pennsylvania but told her parents at the age of four she wanted to be a gypsy when she grew up. She has a soft spot for babies, puppies and 90s Grunge music and believes in Bigfoot and aliens. She started writing at the age of twelve and prides herself on making her characters larger than life and her sex scenes hotter than hot.

She burst into the world of publishing in 2010 after having five beautiful bambinos and figuring they were old enough to get their own snacks while she pounds away at the keys. In her not-so-spare time, she is fur-mommy to a Labradoodle named Daisy Hasselhoff.

Find More Books by Em Petrova at empetrova.com

Other Titles by Em Petrova

Other Titles by Em Petrova

SEAL Team Blackout
SHATTERED TIES Bishop's Story
RUTHLESS PROTECTION Sparrow's Story
MERCILESS SURVIVAL Ramsey's Story
SAVAGE PAWN Gunnison's Story
REBEL MISSION Frost's Story
WICKED INSTINCT Lachlan's Story
FINAL TARGET Mustang's Story
DIRTY JUSTICE Apollo's Story
SWEET REFUGE Lena and Overstreet's Story

WEST Protection
HIGH-STAKES COWBOY Noah's Story
RESCUED BY THE COWBOY Ross's Story
GUARDED BY THE COWBOY Boone's Story
COWBOY CONSPIRACY THEORY Mathias's Story
COWBOY IN THE CROSSHAIRS Silas's Story
PROTECTED BY THE COWBOY Josiah's Story
BRAVO TANGO COWBOY Corrine and Panic's Story
BREAKING IN THE COWBOY Casey's Story
SHIELDED BY THE COWBOY McCoy's Story

CLOSE RANGE COWBOY Landon's Story
ZERO DARK COWBOY Judd's Story
TOP SECRET COWBOY Jace's Story
COWBOY UNDER SEIGE Jaren's Story
COWBOY BREAKING POINT Quaide's Story
LONG ARM OF THE COWBOY Lexis's Story
SHOTGUN WEDDING COWBOY Julius's Story
JUSTICE FOR THE COWBOY Jennings's Story

MT Ops
MOUNTAIN PROTECTOR
MOUNTAIN DEFENDER
MOUNTAIN KEEPER

Xtreme Ops
HITTING XTREMES
TO THE XTREME
XTREME BEHAVIOR
XTREME AFFAIRS
XTREME MEASURES
XTREME PRESSURE
XTREME LIMITS
Xtreme Ops Alaska Search and Rescue
NORTH OF LOVE
XTREME RULES

Crossroads
BAD IN BOOTS
CONFIDENT IN CHAPS
COCKY IN A COWBOY HAT
SAVAGE IN A STETSON
SHOW-OFF IN SPURS

Dark Falcons MC
DIXON
TANK
PATRIOT
DIESEL
BLADE

The Guard
HIS TO SHELTER
HIS TO DEFEND
HIS TO PROTECT

Moon Ranch
TOUGH AND TAMED
SCREWED AND SATISFIED
CHISELED AND CLAIMED

Ranger Ops

AT CLOSE RANGE
WITHIN RANGE
POINT BLANK RANGE
RANGE OF MOTION
TARGET IN RANGE
OUT OF RANGE

Knight Ops Series
ALL KNIGHTER
HEAT OF THE KNIGHT
HOT LOUISIANA KNIGHT
AFTER MIDKNIGHT
KNIGHT SHIFT
ANGEL OF THE KNIGHT
O CHRISTMAS KNIGHT

Wild West Series
SOMETHING ABOUT A LAWMAN
SOMETHING ABOUT A SHERIFF
SOMETHING ABOUT A BOUNTY HUNTER
SOMETHING ABOUT A MOUNTAIN MAN

Operation Cowboy Series
KICKIN' UP DUST
SPURS AND SURRENDER

Rope 'n Ride Series
BUCK
RYDER
RIDGE
WEST
LANE
WYNONNA

The Dalton Boys
COWBOY CRAZY Hank's story
COWBOY BARGAIN Cash's story
COWBOY CRUSHIN' Witt's story
COWBOY SECRET Beck's story
COWBOY RUSH Kade's Story
COWBOY MISTLETOE a Christmas novella
COWBOY FLIRTATION Ford's story
COWBOY TEMPTATION Easton's story
COWBOY SURPRISE Justus's story
COWGIRL DREAMER Gracie's story
COWGIRL MIRACLE Jessamine's story
COWGIRL HEART Kezziah's story

Single Titles and Boxes
THE BOOT KNOCKERS RANCH BOX SET
THE DALTON BOYS BOX SET
SINFUL HEARTS

JINGLE BOOTS
A COWBOY FOR CHRISTMAS
FULL RIDE

Firehouse 5 Series
ONE FIERY NIGHT
CONTROLLED BURN
SMOLDERING HEARTS

Hardworking Heroes Novellas

EM PETROVA
WWW.EMPETROVA.COM

Made in the USA
Columbia, SC
22 May 2023

17146139R00124